Louisa Heaton lives on Hayling Island, Hampshire, with her husband, four children and a small zoo. She has worked in various roles in the health industry—most recently four years as a Community First Responder, answering 999 calls. When not writing Louisa enjoys other creative pursuits, including reading, quilting and patchwork—usually instead of the things she *ought* to be doing!

Also by Louisa Heaton

Christmas with the Single Dad
Reunited by Their Pregnancy Surprise
Their Double Baby Gift
Pregnant with His Royal Twins
A Child to Heal Them
Saving the Single Dad Doc
Their Unexpected Babies
The Prince's Cinderella Doc
Pregnant by the Single Dad Doc
Healed by His Secret Baby

Discover more at millsandboon.co.uk.

THE ICELANDIC DOC'S BABY SURPRISE

LOUISA HEATON

MILLS & BOON

First published in Great Britain 2020
by Mills & Boon, an imprint of HarperCollins*Publishers*
1 London Bridge Street, London, SE1 9GF
www.harpercollins.co.uk

HarperCollins*Publishers*
1st Floor, Watermarque Building, Ringsend Road
Dublin 4, Ireland

Large Print edition 2021

© 2020 Louisa Heaton

ISBN: 978-0-263-28765-3

MIX
Paper from
responsible sources
FSC
www.fsc.org   FSC C007454

This book is produced from independently certified FSC™ paper to ensure responsible forest management. For more information visit www.harpercollins.co.uk/green.

Printed and bound in Great Britain
by CPI Group (UK) Ltd, Croydon, CR0 4YY

For all of the strong women
who inspire me to be my best.

xxx

CHAPTER ONE

DR MERRY BELL shook her head in dismay at the music coming from the taxi driver's radio. Cheesy Christmas music being played *here*? In Iceland?

She'd expected it in England. They'd been playing Christmas tunes on the radio since mid-November and she'd stopped listening to the radio in her car just because of that fact. Instead she'd loaded up a few podcasts and listened to those. Or audiobooks. Anything but the false jollity that the season brought with it.

It really was crazy the way people got so idiotic as December crept nearer. There was no appeal in it for her. Christmas only served to remind her of the worst mistake of her life.

Coming here to Iceland, somehow she'd expected something different. Traditional Icelandic music, maybe...

Merry stared resentfully out of the window of the taxi that was making slow progress up a snow-lined mountain pass. Tall banks of snow lay on either side and the white stuff was coming down heavily, in thick, large flakes, silently hitting the windshield before being pushed to one side by wipers that appeared to be struggling in the blizzard that had hit just after her plane had arrived in Reykjavik.

You didn't get to see snow like this in England.

Maybe I should try to appreciate it?

But she couldn't. Her mind was on other matters. Her destination, and the man at the centre of that destination—Dr Kristjan Gunnarsson. Now, there was a man who made her feel all hot and bothered. Made her blood pulse at an accelerated pace. A man who could melt all this snow just by sending one searing look its way.

Even now just the thought of seeing him again, of having to stand in front of him and tell him her news, made her thrum with a heat that was triple X-rated.

She thought of the last time they'd met. The last time she'd seen him he'd been naked in her bed, calling her back to him with a twinkle in those ice-blue eyes of his and a little curl of his beckoning finger.

Hawaii.

They'd both got carried away that last night. She'd thrown caution to the non-existent wind and decided to just let go and take a chance— after all, she'd never have to see the man ever again!

That had been the plan, anyway.

Before the medical conference had even started she'd gone for a walk on the beach and seen him emerging from the sea in a pair of trunks that had clung to his muscular thighs, water dripping down his broad, sculptured form.

She'd actually gasped to herself. James Bond and Mr Darcy emerging from the water had nothing on this guy! Watching Kristjan had been like watching the sea god Poseidon himself appearing from the waves. He'd run his hand over his hair, wiped the water from his face, and then he'd stood there, watching her, waiting for her to say something.

She'd wanted to say something cute, something amusing, but the only thing to come out of her mouth had been, 'The water looks good.'

And he'd replied, 'Just the water?' with a charming accent she hadn't quite been able to distinguish and a smirk that ought to have had a health warning attached to it.

Warning! May cause hot flushes and a racing heart.

That had been the start of it. The flirtation. She'd hoped that maybe he was just a tourist— but, no, he'd been part of the conference. He'd even been one of the speakers...talking about the social determinants of childhood health.

She'd sat in that room, watching him on the podium, his grey suit clinging in all the right places, his long blond hair restrained in a Viking plait down his back, and *tried* to concentrate on his words. But all she'd been able to think of was that first image she'd had of him...the shape of his well-hewn muscles, the droplets of water that had adhered to his pectorals, the way those trunks of his had clung to his body and what she would have given to run her fingers over his hot flesh...

Merry had never considered herself a lustful person, but looking at him, listening to him, had made her feel that way—naughty and excited, and her body had tingled in all the right places.

When his talk had been over her feet had propelled her towards him, to thank him for an inspiring talk, and he had turned to greet her, those sapphire eyes looking into her own molten brown ones, and she had felt like melting into a puddle under the intense heat of his gaze.

He'd bought her a drink. And then another. And she'd learned that they were both parentless. She'd been abandoned in a cardboard box outside the local vicar's house before some carol singers had arrived and found her there. That was how she'd got her name—Merry. And the paramedic who had been called out to her, who'd held her in the ambulance, his surname had been Bell. It had seemed apt, what with it being Christmas…

It hadn't been a great name for going through school, though. The jokes had never ended.

Kristjan's start in life had not been so terrible. He'd started out with a family but had lost his parents at an early age and ended up in the care system.

But sitting in that bar, sharing stories, had

bonded them in a way she'd not expected. Before she'd known what she was doing she had told him her room number, and that had been the end—*the beginning?*—of that.

The hottest night of her life—and not just because they'd been in the tropics.

When she'd been married, sex had been quick and perfunctory and only for her husband's pleasure—and then he would fall asleep. With Kristjan it had been completely different, and he had made her body *sing*. Had shown her that her pleasure was just as important as his own.

Just thinking, even now, of how he had made her body feel, she experienced a feeling of heat and a blush stemming up from her very core. Thank goodness it was night-time, and the driver couldn't see the colour in her cheeks. Couldn't see as she shifted in her seat to try and pretend that she was just making herself more comfortable.

What would Kristjan say when he saw her? Would he be happy to see her? Or was she about to find out that the man she'd thought was impossibly single was actually married, with a wife he'd forgotten to tell her about? A *life* that she was about to turn upside down?

Because how could a man like that be single? It wasn't possible, was it? Unless he was one of those men who enjoyed his many conquests of women without any of the complications of a committed relationship?

Either way, he was about to get the news of a lifetime. Once she got to her B&B she'd change, shower, have something to eat and get an early night. Tomorrow she would see him. Tomorrow she would tell him and then be on her way.

She would have done the right thing. The moral thing. She neither wanted nor needed his interference in the matter, and if this was just about her she wouldn't be here at all.

Merry frowned, trying to see beyond the blizzard outside, trying to make some sense of the lights she saw in the distance. The taxi driver had collected her from the airport and told her that the trip to Snowy Peak was about two hours. All this time she'd seen nothing outside the window but a dark whiteness.

She only knew where he worked. He'd told her as they'd lain facing each other on soft white pillows, as his hand slid down her side into the dip of her stomach and then over the swell of her hip and thigh, before pulling her close, pressing her against him and beginning again.

She knew what she wanted to do. She wanted to keep it. But she didn't need *him*. She didn't need anyone and was more than happy to be everything this baby needed. Her child would not be left in a cardboard box, the way she had been. The only cardboard boxes her child would get close to would be the ones they used to play with. To make forts out of…or dens… or castles.

She suddenly became aware that the taxi had come to a stop. Merry frowned and leant forward. 'Something wrong?' Because it didn't look as if they'd arrived anywhere! The road ahead was hidden by the still falling snow and all around them it was dark.

'The road is too dangerous now. You must walk from here.'

She looked out at the snow, and then down at her trainers. All her luggage was in the boot of the car. It had been bad enough manhandling it through an airport, never mind up a mountain. Surely he wasn't serious?

'You are joking?'

The dark-haired driver turned around in his seat to face her. 'I do not joke. I am serious. I turn around here. Go back before road is impassable.'

'But…we're in the middle of nowhere!'

'Snowy Peak is top of this mountain. Ten minutes.'

'If it's just ten minutes then you can take me! I'm *paying* you to take me there.'

'Too steep like this. Snow too thick. Very dangerous. You must go on foot.'

Merry was exasperated. 'Seriously?'

'You want to crash? Fall down mountain? We do that if I drive you.'

She could see he was serious. She hadn't noticed the slow, steady climb of the car because she'd been so busy thinking about meeting up with Kristjan. But now she could see they were at an upward angle and that the road ahead, though thick with snow, looked sloped.

She could see a glow at the crest of the hill. Lights? From Snowy Peak? She knew the main hospital was there. Somewhere, anyway. And if it was only ten minutes…

She reluctantly thrust some money at the driver and he got out to help her get her bags from the boot.

The snow was coming down even more strongly, cold and wet, hitting her face. And, now she was out in it, it didn't seem as pretty as it had from inside the nice warm car. She was wearing the wrong shoes, the wrong clothes. And her suitcase wheels would be useless in the snow!

'Are you sure about this?' she yelled at the driver above the sound of the whistling wind.

'Yes. You go. Soon it will be too heavy.'

This wasn't too heavy already?

Merry slung one bag over her shoulder and tried to drag her suitcase behind her as she made her way up the road. The ice and snow beat against her face and hair and she could feel the cold soaking into her toes and clothes as she made slow headway through the storm. The thick tights she wore underneath her dress might as well have been the very lowest denier, because her legs felt bare in this intense cold.

Behind her, she saw the taillights of the taxi

disappearing into the darkness of the night, and she swore before turning once again and plodding her way through the knee-high snow. She wanted to blame the driver, but even she could see how deep the snow was getting. Without a snowplough on the front of his vehicle, it was amazing that he'd been able to get this far as it was.

She was cold, and wet, and her legs were aching. But just when she thought she couldn't stand another moment in this weather she made the crest of the hill.

Spread out before her were the lights of Snowy Peak, warm yellow and white globes, and to one side a huge building that she saw was called the Snowy Peak Children's Hospital. She let out an exhausted breath on seeing it and trudged towards it, feeling relief that the taxi driver hadn't been kidding, even if he *had* just left her on the side of a snowy mountain at night.

With no idea of how to get to the B&B, she headed towards the hospital, a haven in the cold and the dark.

As she walked through the sliding doors, feeling a welcoming and pleasant gust of warm air from the heater above, she saw all eyes turn to her and realised just what she must look like…

Dr Kristjan Gunnarsson had been more than happy to push Aron's wheelchair towards the hospital shop. The little boy had waited days since his spinal surgery to get his first taste of a particular chocolate-covered fudge bar that had small bits of black liquorice suspended in its filling.

It wasn't something that they served on the hospital's healthy menu, and Kristjan had promised Aron a bar as soon as he was able to transfer himself to a wheelchair and stay in it for one hour without pain. That day had been today, and he'd never been prouder. In fact, Aron wanted to stay in the wheelchair until his mum arrived that night, so she could see him in it, too. He wanted it to be a surprise.

Now, with Aron chewing on his chocolatey snack, Kristjan was wheeling him back through the entrance foyer, towards the lifts that would take them back up to Aron's floor, when he became aware of the woman who had just trudged through the entrance doors, wheeling a snow-topped suitcase behind her. She'd stopped, propped the suitcase upright and was shaking the snow off her shoulders and her dark brown hair.

She looked miserably cold and wet and she was wearing totally the wrong things for winter in Iceland. Trainers, green tights, a yellow woollen dress and a short jacket. Only one woman he knew wore crazy clothes like that, but the last time he'd seen her she'd been in Hawaii, even though she lived in Brighton, England.

But now it would seem she was here.

Merry. *Dr* Merry Bell.

She hadn't spotted him yet, and he took a moment to try and slow his breathing and appraise her. Her hair looked longer. He didn't remember it being that long the time they'd stood in the shower together, she with her hands up against the tiles and her back to him, when he'd lifted her hair away from her neck to kiss her hot skin...

Longing burned through him at the memory of that night and one morning they had spent together. She'd been unlike any woman he had ever met, and he'd left Hawaii—and her—with fond and extremely hot memories, knowing that it was probably for the best that she lived in another country.

She had been the first woman in his life who had made him yearn for more, but he didn't do full-on relationships—ever—and committing to more than one night with her would have broken all the rules he held himself accountable to. The rules that kept everyone at a distance—the way he liked them to be. Because then there would be no more pain. If he didn't get close and emotionally involved, he wouldn't have to face the losses that would come later.

But Hawaii had been—what? Roughly three months ago? What was she doing here? Was she here to work? There was a vacancy, but as far as he'd understood the hospital had chosen to wait until after Christmas to advertise.

He longed to go over to her and find out why she was here. As if his yearning had called out to her their eyes met and he felt the punch of it hit him in the gut.

And somewhere *lower*.

Her lips parted slightly, as if she was on the verge of saying something, but then she bit her lip and it was all he could do not to self-implode on the spot. He took a moment to gather himself, and used it to pretend he was just checking the brake on Aron's wheelchair.

Then he said, 'Excuse me, Aron, I won't be a moment.' And headed over to Merry.

As he got closer he could see the snow crystals still melting in her dark hair, and the way her make-up had smudged around her eyes, making them look smoky and sultry. He slowed as he got closer, taking his time to soak her up. She looked as if she needed a nice hot shower, and he could think of nothing better than taking her upstairs to the staff area, where there was a bathroom, and helping her off with her clothes. But he was on duty, and now was not the time for a seduction.

Was she aware that the outlines of her cold, peaked nipples were showing through her woollen dress?

He raised his eyes back up to her face. 'Hello, Merry.'

He could see she was just as disturbed by his presence as he was by hers, and it pleased him. He watched her cheeks flush with colour, and she pulled her jacket closed around her, as if it were a suit of armour.

'Hello, Kristjan.'

CHAPTER TWO

OKAY, SO SHE hadn't imagined it. Kristjan really was as stunning as she remembered. Tall and broad, muscular and strong. And looking just as luscious in clothes as he did out of them.

Don't think of him naked. That isn't helping!

She squeezed her eyes shut to try and dispel the image, but it was like trying to ignore an elephant in the room. You couldn't help but look at the huge grey creature. Only *her* elephant looked like a Viking out of time. He would look just as comfortable in a horned helmet, swinging a massive battle-axe, as he did in the bespoke suit, and that waistcoat he wore just emphasised his neat, flat stomach, under which she *knew* lay a set of perfectly moulded abs...

She forced herself to look elsewhere, and noticed that the hospital had a huge decorated Christmas tree in the centre of the entrance foyer and that 'White Christmas' was being piped out of hidden speakers.

Christmas. *Ugh.*

'To what do I owe the…pleasure?' asked Kristjan.

She could feel his eyes raking over her, and she wished again that she'd worn something a bit more suitable. She yanked once more at both sides of her jacket, to try and pull it closed. She hadn't expected to come straight from the airport and meet Kristjan. She'd expected the taxi to take her to the B&B she'd booked first, so she could settle in, get changed, and then meet Kristjan on *her* terms. She hadn't planned to be wearing her travelling clothes.

'The taxi driver made me walk up the last bit of the mountain. He was meant to be taking me to a B&B. I thought someone here might direct me to it…' She hoped she sounded as unbothered by him as she hoped.

Kristjan looked outside, assessing the weather. 'You came up the mountain in *this*?' he sounded angry.

'I didn't really have a choice in the matter. So…the Kerling B&B…?'

'This storm will go on for some time now, and I can't let you go outside in those cold, wet clothes—'

'You can't *let* me?' *Who did he think he was?*

'You can sleep here tonight.'

Sleep here? In the hospital? 'No. I can't.'

'There are plenty of beds in the on-call rooms.'

And she knew exactly what happened in on-call rooms.

She felt herself flush once again, knowing she did not want Kristjan to know where she was sleeping. He might expect something from her. A continuation of their bedtime adventures. And that wasn't what she was here for! In no way did she want or need any relationship with this man. Even if she *had* briefly entertained the idea of him hearing her news and sweeping her off her feet into the sunset, like men did in the movies.

No, he'd been fun for one night, when she'd thought she'd never see him again, and now it was more complicated than that she didn't need him making it worse, with his blue eyes and good intentions and beautifully honed muscles…

'I'd rather make my way to the B&B.'

'Why?' He looked amused and leaned in, whispering, 'You think I'm going to sneak into your on-call room in the middle of the night?'

She remembered how he'd whispered into her ear just what he was going to do to her that night in Hawaii, and she shivered at the memory.

'You're cold. Let's at least get you warm and dry and into a change of clothes.'

That *did* sound like a good idea, she had to admit. The clothes she had on were soaked, and she was freezing, and that couldn't be good for her condition. Not that he knew that. Not yet.

Reluctantly, she found herself agreeing. 'All right…'

He smiled and stepped forward to take her suitcase, then led her over to the lifts, where Aron waited. 'Aron, this is Dr Bell. Dr Bell—Aron Mikkelsson.'

The little boy in the wheelchair had chocolate at the sides of his mouth.

She smiled. 'Hello, Aron.'

'You are English?' Aron asked.

She was impressed that he knew some English and was willing to try it out on her. 'I am.'

'You know the Queen?' he asked, with excitement in his voice.

She laughed and shook her head. 'I'm afraid not, no.'

'Oh. Okay…'

She glanced at Kristjan as the doors to the lift opened and deliberately stood on the opposite side of Aron's wheelchair to create a distance between them once they were inside.

Kristjan pressed the button to take them up to the fourth floor of the hospital and they rode in silence.

She tried her hardest not to look at him. But her body was in perfect awareness of his proximity. Soon she couldn't stand it any more, and just had to have a quick glance.

Then she looked down at Aron and smiled. 'So, Aron, why are you here in the hospital?'

'He had an operation,' Kristjan answered.

'Oh?'

Aron just smiled, licking the chocolate from around his mouth.

'Removal of a malignant glial tumour,' Kristjan explained.

She nodded, then smiled again at Aron, because it was easier to look at the child than it was the man. The extremely virile man...

A quick glance at the left hand holding the handle of Aron's wheelchair showed no ring. Did that mean anything? He'd not been expecting her, so if he normally wore one he wouldn't have thought to hide it. This had to be normal, right? But not every married man wore a ring, and she had no idea if the traditions regarding marriage were different here in Iceland. Perhaps the men here didn't wear rings? Who knew?

The lift doors pinged open, revealing a corridor filled with tinsel and pictures on the wall of reindeer leaping through the snow and candy canes hanging from branches filled with fairy lights. The nurses' desk had a miniature Christmas tree, and more tinsel around the noticeboard, and in a corner by the linen cupboard was a stack of presents that almost reached the ceiling.

'Wait here. I'll just escort Aron back to his bed and get him comfortable.'

She nodded and watched Kristjan walk away, pushing the small boy's wheelchair. It felt odd to see him in this environment. She'd only ever seen him at the conference, presenting—or naked, of course. She'd almost forgotten he was a paediatric doctor, like her.

As they moved away she heard him say something to the boy. They both laughed and she smiled without realising it, watching them. He clearly got on well with the young lad, and she took a couple of steps forward so she could watch through the safety glass as he helped Aron out of his chair and safely back into bed. He passed Aron a book from his bedside, said something else, and then ruffled the boy's hair.

This was a different side to him, and it intrigued her greatly to see him with the boy. But that intrigue disturbed her. It shouldn't matter that he was great with kids. So she turned away and deliberately went over to the nurses' station, pretending to look through a bunch of leaflets that she thought were about vaccinations, so he wouldn't catch her watching him.

He had to be wondering why she was here. Was it too late to pretend that she was here for some other reason and then just go home again? He would never have to know! They'd never run into each other. He lived in Iceland.

She in England—Brighton. The chances of them ever meeting again were slim…

But she knew she couldn't do that. Not to him and not to her baby. She had been abandoned and left without any parents. Growing up, she would have killed to know *something* about who her parents were! This baby in her belly had a father, and she knew *who* he was and *where* he was. Her child deserved to know its dad, too. Even if they hardly ever got to see one another.

That was how this was going to play out. That was her plan and she expected nothing else. She would tell him about the baby, and that she was going to keep it, and then she would go home. Start a life with her child back in Brighton. Her baby would know who it came from. Its mum and its dad. Her baby would have what she'd never had. And if her child ever wanted to go to Iceland… Well, they'd cross that bridge if they ever came to it.

She sensed his presence behind her before she turned to look at him.

'So…' he said.

'So…' She gave him a brief smile.

Now was not the time. Not like this. She was

a mess, and shivering, and he was on duty. He deserved to hear this news when he had the time and the ability to sit and listen properly. Right now, she just wanted to get out of her wet clothes.

And into his arms? Imagine how good it would feel to press yourself against his hot, solid body...

'You mentioned somewhere I could get changed?' she said.

He gave a nod. 'Of course. Here—let me take that.' And he grabbed her wheeled suitcase and led the way.

She followed after him, admiring his restraint, not asking her questions. But, then again, he'd been good at holding off his own pleasure, making sure she was pleasured first... A shiver rippled down her spine and she rubbed at her arms to rid herself of the goosebumps that prickled over her skin.

He brought her to a door marked Aðeins Starfsfólk, pushing it open. Inside was what was obviously a staffroom, with lockers and a small kitchen area in one corner, and another door leading to a bathroom.

'Shower is through there. Want any help?'

She stared at him, her face flushing with heat, remembering that shower taken with him. 'No! Most definitely not!'

He laughed. 'I'm joking, Merry. I'm on duty. Relax.'

She let out a breath. Of course he was joking! She should have realised.

He grabbed a piece of paper off the small coffee table and scribbled a number on it. 'This is my mobile number. Get one of the nurses to contact me when you're done.'

She took the paper, but knew she wouldn't call him. Once she'd showered and changed she would be asking the nurses to direct her to her B&B. Then she would return tomorrow, to tell him about the baby.

'Thank you.'

'You're very welcome.'

He smiled at her for a moment and she allowed herself that moment to look into his eyes and wonder what it would be like to be more to him than a moment in time. To let herself be swept off her feet and into his bed again and who knew what afterwards?

But the moment passed as he pushed her case towards her hands.

'It's good to see you, Merry.'

She gave him a brief smile, then looked down and away. When she looked up again he'd gone, and the smack of disappointment that washed over her left her feeling confused and disturbed and lost all at once.

But Merry headed into the bathroom, closing and locking the door firmly behind her.

Rejuvenated, showered, warm and dry, she collected her things before heading out of the staff room, intent on asking a nurse for directions to her B&B.

But when she came hurrying out of the bathroom, ready to make her escape, she found Kristjan sitting on one of the couches, reading a newspaper that he put down at her appearance. He tilted his head to one side to look at her appraisingly and he smiled, standing, stretching to his full height.

She felt like a little elf before him. A naughty elf who had been caught trying to scurry out of the grotto without being seen by Santa Claus.

'You're here,' she said accusingly.

'I am.'

'But you're meant to be working.'

'And you're meant to be calling me. But I

had a feeling you were going to leave without doing so—am I right?'

She coloured.

'What's going on, Merry? Why are you here?'

He genuinely seemed to want to know. Had he been worrying about it ever since he'd left her to take a shower? Could he not bear the thought of not knowing the answer?

She owed it to him. Why keep him waiting?

Because I didn't think it would happen like this.

She'd imagined sitting down with him in a coffee shop, or something—somewhere public, where neither of them could make a scene. Where she couldn't allow herself to fall into his arms. Because these last few weeks she'd been filled with a dizzying array of moods and emotions and she wasn't fully able to trust her body right now—*or* its responses.

One alarming change in particular had been to her sex drive. It hadn't taken her long to notice that it seemed to be on overdrive—she'd noticed every good-looking man at the airport and on the plane over here. And now she was with *him*. The man who had caused all this.

She was aware of everything about him.
How he stood. His curious smile. The way
his mouth was slightly curled. The way his
hands sat on his hips as he stood there, looking at her with questioning eyes.

'I'm here to see you,' she said.

His eyes darkened. Was he pleased by her
response? Or bothered by it?

'Why?' he asked. 'What we had in Hawaii
was amazing, but it was finished when you
walked out of your hotel room wearing that
pretty blue dress.'

He remembered what she'd worn? That was
nice…

'It's not finished.'

Kristjan smiled. 'Really? How so?' His voice
was curious. 'I don't do long-term relationships, Merry. However, if you're interested
in pursuing a purely sexual relationship, then
I'm—'

'I'm pregnant, Kristjan. With your baby,' she
added unnecessarily. Because what else would
she be pregnant with?

She swallowed hard, awaiting his response,
watching as myriad emotions played over his
face. She saw shock. Surprise. Disbelief. He

blinked, turned away, then instantly turned back again, as if he wanted to ask her a question, but nothing would come out of his mouth.

She'd never seen him unsure of anything. In all the time she had spent with him he had been surefooted, in control, had known exactly what he was doing at all times. This was a man who had stood at a podium in front of hundreds of other doctors and given his presentation assuredly, never faltering, never nervous—a man who'd had his audience in the palm of his hand. He had always seemed to know what was happening, and how, but now, in this very instant, he was floundering, and she could see how difficult he was finding that.

He was responding with the same emotions that she had felt when she'd watched that stick turn pink in her bathroom at home. Sheer disbelief…denial of the truth that had been right in front of her!

She was glad it wasn't easy for him, because it hadn't been easy for her.

And now he knew.

Her job was done.

I can go.

CHAPTER THREE

KRISTJAN COULD HEAR the cold wind whistling around the corner of the hospital, and through the window behind her he saw thick flakes of snow being blown this way, then that. She looked like an angel standing there, with that wintry backdrop and the tinsel around the window.

A very small angel.

Pregnant. With his baby.

His baby.

He felt a rush of emotions. Some that he could identify, others not so much. They rushed past so fast, just like the snow in the storm—there one minute, gone the next.

Never in his life had he expected a complication such as this. He loved kids—loved helping kids, making them better and sending them home—but he'd never thought to have one of his own.

Having a child meant having a relationship,

making a commitment, and that was the sort of thing he had never aspired to—because wanting something like that opened you up to a whole new world of hurt, and the world was tough enough anyway. Being with someone else, in a relationship, meant knowing that you could lose them, and he'd already lost more than he cared to.

Only now—now that it had happened and Merry was standing before him, awaiting his reaction—he felt a stirring of something that he'd left well alone for a very long time. A feeling that he had kept locked away since he was very young, as soon as he had been capable of making such a decision.

His baby. *His.*

She had to be three months along. Heading into the second trimester. He looked down at her abdomen, but it was still flat. He watched her cover her abdomen with her hands, almost as if she could protect the baby from his stare.

'You want to keep it?'

He knew it was a horrible question to ask, but he figured she'd come all this way to tell him, so the likelihood that she did was strong.

But he needed to know for sure. Needed her to say the words.

A look flashed in those chocolate eyes of hers. 'Yes. I do. I am. I need nothing from you, Kristjan. I just thought I'd do the right thing and let you know. And now that I have I can go home again.'

He frowned. Go home again? She had to be kidding? Down the mountain? In this? And they'd sorted nothing out. Nothing at all! What was going to happen in the future? With money. Visitation rights etc.

Why am I thinking about any of that? It's not like I'm going to be a full-time father. She lives in another country!

And that thought burrowed its way down into his soul like a root. It took hold of the desire he'd once hidden, then spread its tendrils throughout him and headed back up to the surface with tender green shoots, its leaves curling open in the light, revealing itself to him.

I can't let her go back. Not yet.

'Not in this weather, you can't. Have you looked outside? The mountain pass will be treacherous. People have died in less severe weather than this.'

She frowned, glancing out of the window. 'For how long? Till tomorrow?'

She really knew nothing about the weather patterns in his country. 'I'd say at least a few days.'

Her face registered her shock at his statement. 'A *few* days? But I'm booked on a flight home in two days!'

'You won't make it. We'll phone the airport and rearrange your flight. Looks like you're going to be here over Christmas.'

'But…'

He could see the thoughts racing over her face as she looked from him to the window and back again. She really was beautiful. Even when she'd looked wet and bedraggled and freezing cold he'd wanted to take her in his arms and pull her towards him. To feel her soft body against his once more. All those feelings he'd stamped down since she left him in Hawaii had come rushing back.

And now that she was looking lost and hopeless… Well, that just made him want to look after her. Only he couldn't. Because she was pregnant with his child. Any move he made to restart what they'd finished in Hawaii would only make her think that they were in some sort of relationship—and they were not.

A baby, though…

That was huge. That was commitment on a grand scale. That was opening himself up to a world of possible heartache and pain, and so far, for most of his life, he'd avoided that by staying single and only having to look after himself. It was a rule that he had kept to for all these years and it had served him well.

Now everything would change. If he got involved in this—*when* he got involved…

'I'll arrange lodgings for you,' he said.

'There won't be anything. It's December. All the rooms in the hotels have been taken by holidaymakers bringing their kids to Wonderland and I got the last room at the B&B, which was only available for two nights. I suppose I could ask them for space on the sofa or the floor after that… They're expecting me.'

Wonderland was the huge purpose-built village next to Snowy Peak that was a Christmas paradise for kids and their families. It brought in a lot of money and was good for the local economy, employing a lot of the locals who lived around the mountain.

He sighed, making a decision without thinking too hard about it. 'Then you'll stay with me.'

'What? I can't do that!'

'I won't have the mother of my child sleeping on a floor. Not when there's a perfectly good bed in my home.'

She looked at him uncertainly. She bit her bottom lip again in a way that was most disconcerting and did strange things to him below his belt.

'A spare bed?' she asked.

'You think I'm asking you to sleep with me?'

'Well...'

'Relax. I'm more than capable of resisting you. You'll be perfectly safe.'

He hoped he sounded believable, because he *knew* how she made him feel, and asking her to stay with him for the next few days was going to be...strange. Especially since he'd never let anyone into his own personal space before. Certainly not someone like her...

'I guess I should say thank you...'

'You're welcome.'

'Am I expected to sit around twiddling my thumbs with nothing to do, though?'

He thought for a moment. 'We can give you privileges at the hospital. You can work here. You're a paediatrician, and we need an extra person over the holidays anyway.'

She nodded. 'All right. I'll feel better if I'm earning my keep. That way I can pay you for board and lodging and food.'

'You don't need to do that.'

'Oh, but I do.'

He stared at her, mulling over the idea of going over to her, pulling her against his chest and kissing her until she stopped talking. He wasn't used to having people argue with him, and her determination to stand on her own two feet and pay him for staying at his place seemed to arouse his desire for her even more—which felt odd to him, because he never went back. He always moved forward.

But he held back. Considered her. The steady resolve in the eyes staring back at him was almost like a challenge. She was no walkover, was she?

'Then let's go see the Chief and get you set up. And then we'll need to get you out of those clothes.' He smiled, determined to put her on the back foot.

'I beg your pardon? These are perfectly acceptable—'

'And get you into some scrubs.' He grinned and held the door open for her. 'After you.'

He watched her as she walked past in her black polo neck and purple skirt, inhaling the scent of her shampoo. It was floral. He couldn't pick out which flower, but it was very nice... soft and gentle. The aroma warmed his senses, making him want to pick up a tress of her hair and inhale it some more.

Only he didn't do that.

He couldn't do that.

Instead, he kept control of his impulses and led her down to the Chief's office.

Merry picked up her first chart, gave it a brief scan, and then headed over to the bed. A really small little girl lay dwarfed in it, surrounded by teddy bears.

'Hello, there. My name is Dr Bell. Can you tell me your name, sweetheart?' She smiled at the little girl. It said on her chart that she was three years old, but she looked half that.

'Tinna.'

'Hello, Tinna!' She reached out to take hold

of the little girl's fingers and shook her hand. 'Nice to meet you. Now…' she looked up at the child's parents, who had stood up on the other side of the bed on her arrival '…can you tell me what's brought you in here, today?'

The parents looked at each other and frowned. Clearly language was going to be a problem here. They obviously knew some basic English, but not much, and as she knew zero Icelandic they were in trouble.

She turned to look for help and saw Kristjan stroll over from another child's bedside.

'Need some assistance?'

Rankled, she pursed her lips. 'There seems to be a language barrier…'

'Ah. Okay. I'll translate for you.'

Which he did.

'She's had a seizure,' he said.

'Okay. When did that happen?'

'Just after dinner.'

'She wasn't choking on her food, or anything like that?'

The parents shook their heads.

'And has she had a seizure before?'

All of this information was in the notes, but she wanted to check and make sure. Sometimes parents remembered extra details on a subsequent retelling of events.

'No.'

'Okay… And how long did it last?'

'Not long. Maybe a half minute?'

'And she has Tay-Sachs?'

Tay-Sachs disease was an inherited condition that mainly affected babies and small children. It had no cure. It would stop the nerves from working, so that young sufferers would lose the ability to use their muscles, reach normal milestones. They would have swallowing difficulties, seizures, and the diseases would eventually be fatal. Not many Tay-Sachs sufferers made it past the age of five.

'Yes.'

'All right.' She put down the chart and sat on the edge of the bed. She smiled at Tinna. 'Okay, so we need to give you some medication to help stop what's happened to you today, so that hopefully it doesn't happen again. Is that all right, Tinna?'

'She wants to know if it will taste bad.'

She smiled. 'No, it won't. How do you feel right now?'

'Okay.'

She turned to the parents. 'Have you noticed any stiffness lately? Any speech problems? Swallowing difficulties?'

'A little.'

'Okay, so some physiotherapy might help her with that. Obviously we want Tinna to keep moving and be strong for as long as she can.'

'Is she going to be in hospital for a long time? They have family visiting, and it's Christmas soon, and they wonder if they'll be able to take her home?'

'I understand.' She turned to the parents once more, speaking low after Kristjan translated. 'I'd like to keep her in for at least twenty-four hours, just to be on the safe side. We'll get her on anti-seizure medication, and if she has no more seizures I don't see why you shouldn't be able to take her home.'

'Thank you, Doctor.'

'You're welcome.' She shook their hands, said goodbye to Tinna, and then went over with Kristjan to the doctors' station. He managed to dwarf everything, due to his size.

He smiled down at her. 'So, how did you feel your first consult went?'

'Fine. I feel really sorry for that little girl,

though. And her poor parents. Tay-Sachs is awful… How do you cope as a parent, knowing your child won't live? It just doesn't seem right.'

She sat down and began inputting her notes, requesting medication for Tinna and asking for her family to be allowed to take her home afterwards. Today had been the child's first seizure, but it would be the start of many. Next time it might be breathing problems that brought Tinna in, and if she got pneumonia…

Merry tried to get rid of the sad thoughts in her head, but she couldn't, and she fought back the sudden sting of tears. A disease like Tay-Sachs was inherited. She had no idea of her own medical history! Her baby could get sick. Merry seemed healthy, and so did Kristjan— for now. But what about what the future held? Neither of them could know and that scared her.

'Are you all right?'

Kristjan's low voice sounded concerned. She forced a bright smile to her face and shrugged. 'I'm fine! What makes you think I'm not?'

'You suddenly stopped typing and you seemed to drift off for a moment.'

'I was thinking.'

'About…?'

What? Did he expect her to share every thought in her head? Who did he think he was? Just because she'd slept with him, and was now carrying his baby, did he think he suddenly had the right to know everything about her? Perhaps agreeing to stay with him was a bad idea. What did she know about him, really?

She couldn't tell him her doubts. How would that sound? *Oh, I don't want to come and stay at yours because you might be an axe murderer.*

'I'm just hungry. It's been a long day.'

He stared at her for a moment. 'Of course. I didn't think. Did you eat on the flight?'

'No, it was just a couple of hours.'

'Let me get you something now.'

'You don't have to do that!' she tried to protest.

But he was already up on his feet and looking taller than ever. He was like a wall—a mountain of a man, with a rugged exterior.

'Of course I do. You don't know where anything is yet. What do you want? Something savoury or something sweet?'

Well, she was so ravenous she would eat anything! 'Both!'

He smiled. 'A woman with a big appetite? I like that.'

Was he still talking about food? She couldn't tell. Not when he was looking at her like that. As if he could eat *her*!

She flushed, feeling the heat in her cheeks, and had to look away, resume her typing.

It was only as he was walking away that she stopped to look at him. His bottom was neatly moulded by his trousers, atop his big, thick, muscular thighs. His plait of hair, tied neatly at the bottom with a twist of leather, reached almost halfway down his broad back.

She remembered what it had felt like to be pressed up against that hard body, and that stirred another type of hunger that she'd hoped she'd got a lid on.

She was going to be working and living with Dr Kristjan Gunnarsson for at least a few days. Maybe even a week! Over Christmas!

It wasn't that she had any family of her own to miss… And Merry figured he was almost her family now. No matter how the future played out, he would always be a part of her life because of their child.

How do I feel about that?

Kristjan was very pretty to look at and lust over, but what else was he? A good doctor, she supposed. He looked after sick kids, and you had to be pretty hard-core to do that. Being a paediatric doctor wasn't for wimps, so he had to be strong emotionally. And he was crazy good in bed...

She cursed and dismissed those intrusive, naughty, X-rated thoughts once again. She needed to be serious about this. Because she wasn't going to let him call the shots. This might be *their* baby, but it was *her* body, and *her* life, and no man—no matter how good-looking or how capable he was of giving her a screaming orgasm—was ever going to be in charge of how her life played out.

She'd given a man the ultimate control before.

No, I didn't give it to him. He took it.

So, there was no way she was going to let Kristjan Gunnarsson take anything away from her.

Ever.

CHAPTER FOUR

KRISTJAN HAD NEVER taken a woman to his home before. It was *his* space and his alone. The fact that he was now opening it up to Merry, the woman who was carrying his child, made him feel very strange indeed…

He watched her as she stepped inside, taking in the huge stone inglenook fireplace that dominated the room, the decorated Christmas tree that stood in the corner beside it. The floor-to-ceiling windows decorated with tiny white lights and the garlands of pine with frosted berries and silver ribbons.

What could he say? He loved Christmas. As his parents had, so many years ago. And he was determined each festive season to honour their memories by outdoing himself from the year before.

That was why he had so much Christmas decoration about the place. The true reason for going overboard at Christmas was that it allowed him to feel closer to them. To remember the way his mother had used to love decorating the tree with him. The way his father had pretended to be Santa.

And to pretend that he wasn't lonely he worked every Christmas in the hospital, with all those kids who didn't get the chance to go home. There was something special and heart-warming about being there at Christmas.

Merry stood by the mantelpiece, looking around her. 'You like Christmas?'

'You don't?'

'Not really.'

He thought everyone loved Christmas. 'Why not?'

She shrugged, but he figured she did know—she just didn't want to tell him. But then again, why would she? They barely knew one another. He'd invited a stranger to his home. To stay with him for a few days. And she was pregnant with his baby! How crazy was that?

'Let me give you the tour once I've lit the fire.'

He got the fire going, and once it was steadily roaring away he got up to show her around—

the kitchen, the bathrooms, the spare bedroom. *His bedroom.*

She stood in the doorway of his bedroom and stared at the king-sized bed. He smiled at her discomfort. 'Don't worry. I don't have any plans to seduce you.'

Merry looked at him. 'Good, because I don't plan on being seduced.'

He walked right up to her, towering over her, and looked down at her beautiful face. 'Let's get you a drink.'

It felt good to be standing so close to her again and, despite his words, he couldn't help but think about what it would be like to kiss her again.

Perhaps she saw the thought in his eyes, because she turned away and headed down the stairs. At the bottom she stood there, fidgeting. 'You have a lovely home.'

He went down to stand beside her. 'Thank you.'

'Even if it *does* look like Santa threw up in here!'

Kristjan laughed. 'You'll get used to it. We Icelanders love Christmas.'

'I'm beginning to understand that.'

She straightened a little figurine he had displayed on a windowsill. It was one of a herd of reindeer, pulling a sled holding a fat Santa and a ginormous sack of presents.

'By the time you leave here you will, too.'

'Oh, I don't think so.'

'No?'

She stared back. 'No.'

'My little ice queen… But we will melt your heart, don't worry.'

'It's fine the way it is. You mentioned a drink? Let me make it—what do you want?'

He raised an eyebrow. He wanted lots of things. Especially as he looked at her standing there, trying her hardest not to be charmed by his home. For instance, he wanted to undress her and make love to her in front of the fireplace. Or take her upstairs and reacquaint her with how good they were together in a shower. Or perhaps take her outside and introduce her to the wonders of a steamy hot tub…

But he also wanted to keep his head on his shoulders. 'Tea will be fine. Thank you.'

He followed her into the kitchen and watched

her get acquainted with where he kept everything. She opened cupboards and drawers, and he found himself smiling at her obvious disgust that all his mugs looked like Christmas puddings because last week he'd swapped them with his normal ones for the festive season.

She looked at the box of teabags and scrunched up her face as she sniffed at it. 'What flavour is this tea?'

'Spiced apple and pear with ginger.'

'Seriously?'

'Wait till you try it. Don't add sugar—add a splash of this.' He passed her some maple syrup.

'You'll rot your teeth.'

'It's just for special occasions.'

'Such as?'

'*Christmas*, Merry. *Christmas*. Come on, tell me—why do you hate it so much? Because you were abandoned at Christmas? I seem to remember you telling me that.'

She passed him his tea and leant back against the kitchen counter. 'I used to love Christmas. The promise of it…what it meant.'

'So what happened?'

She shook her head, as if she couldn't quite believe she was going to tell him her story. 'A guy happened.'

He nodded in understanding. As he'd suspected. And that only gave strength as to his own reasons for staying single. *You let people in, you let yourself become vulnerable and people hurt you.* It always happened. Staying out of relationships was definitely the way to go.

But then he looked down at her belly. Thought about the baby growing there. He couldn't stay out of *that* relationship, could he? He might keep to himself, but he was a decent person and he would take care of his responsibilities.

'I apologise on behalf of all menfolk.' He smiled and raised his cup to her as if in a toast.

'And now another bloke has got me pregnant and I'm going to be a single mother.'

'It takes two, Merry. And we did use protection.'

'I know that!'

'You plan on staying in England?'

She laughed. 'You expect me to move to Iceland?'

'No.'

Yes.

The idea of knowing he would have a child in this world but not be able to see it was disturbing to him now that he thought about it. It had been a long time since he'd had a family, and now…

He smiled at himself—at the craziness of the situation. Just this morning it had been life as usual—no relationships, no commitments—and he had been happy. And tonight…? Tonight he was worrying about which country his child would live in, because he wanted to see it every day.

I do. I want to see it every day.

It would never have been his decision to be a father. He'd never wanted to get involved with anyone—that had always been his modus operandi. But now that it was a possibility—was *real*—he was surprised to discover he had opinions on the matter.

He was an all-in kind of a guy when he did something. He was fully committed to his work at the hospital. Being a paediatric doctor was his life! So the idea of only half-heartedly being a father was not one he could consolidate in his mind. That wasn't him. Sending money and birthday cards would not be enough. He wanted to be *involved.*

'Good. Because my life is in England,' Merry said.

'It could be here.'

'In the land of ice and snow? I don't think so!'

'You'll grow to love it. Trust me.'

'I'm not uprooting my entire life to move here because a *man* wants me to.'

'Then do it because the father of your child has asked you to.' He stared hard at her, wanting to show her he was serious.

She stared back at him and he could see that she was frightened. It was written all over her face. He didn't like seeing her scared. He didn't like seeing anyone feel that way. He fought the urge to cross over to her and pull her close, because he knew she didn't need that right now and would not appreciate it. She would view it as him trying to press his wishes on her.

A man had hurt her. Badly. He didn't know exactly how, but he did know that if he stood any chance of having his child in his life he needed to persuade this woman who stirred his blood that she could have a life *here*. He couldn't go to England. Iceland ran through his veins! He had history here. Roots. And... and it was a good place to raise a child.

I'm crazy to even consider this!

But he knew he had to.

Kristjan had lost the family he'd once had, and he had often yearned to have *someone*. When he had watched those other kids at the school gates running into their parents' loving arms. Watched them get scooped up and have kisses planted on their cheeks. He'd had that. Once.

His aunt and uncle had taken him in for a little while, but it had never been the same. They'd never wanted kids, and to suddenly find themselves parents had been a difficult transition for them.

They'd tried so *hard*. But he had known he was a burden to them. An extra struggle, both financial and emotional. He had felt like a spare part, and he'd been so desperate for love he had been left feeling angry. He'd rebelled as a teenager. That hadn't gone down well! Getting into trouble over silly things… he'd ended up in care. But that anger had fuelled him to stand alone and live his life *his* way.

He wanted more for his own child.

His child would have its father waiting for him or her at the school gates, and Kristjan knew he would be the type of father to scoop his child up into his arms and smother it with kisses!

'Let me prove it to you,' he said.

'Prove what?'

'That you and the baby could have a good life here in this country.'

She cradled her Christmas pudding mug in both hands and stared at him. Considered him. 'You *want* to be part of its life?'

'I do.'

Had she heard his voice waver? *He* had. But this *meant* something to him. Even with the short time he'd known about it, he knew he needed to be a part of this baby's life. 'Give me until the New Year. If you're not convinced, then go home to England and we'll sort something out.'

She stared at him for an age and he couldn't read her. Would she give him this chance? Would she stay?

He had no idea right now just how exactly he was going to prove to her that it would be worth her moving to another country on a permanent basis, but he knew he had to give it a try.

It was Christmas! The season of goodwill to all men and women—and babies. She *had* to give him a chance, right? She had to give him a chance to know his child. To *love* his child. Every day.

'All right.'

'All right?'

'I'll give you until the road clears, then I'm going. Understood?'

He nodded, knowing that the season and the weather were on his side. At this time of year most of the tourists has already arrived, well in advance of Christmas, and once the roads were impassable they would be like that for a long time. If he kept her busy with work, and showed her all the wonders of this place, then maybe she wouldn't have time to check weather reports and road conditions because she'd be falling in love.

He just had to show her the truth and the beauty of the place.

He would make her fall in love with being here.

A knock on the bedroom door had her slowly waking from a deep slumber. She'd never slept so well before. This bed was unbelievable! The mattress wasn't too hard, the blankets were thick and warm, and on top there was a pure white faux fur-lined topper.

After going into her room last night to settle down, she'd put on her pyjamas and then run her fingers through the topper as she passed by, unable to believe that this luxurious bedroom was to be hers! And the best part was it didn't look like a Christmas grotto in here. Kristjan's guest room had been minimally decorated—and that said a lot, considering how the rest of the house looked.

There were thick white candles on the windowsill, a garland of holly over the small fireplace that contained a log burner, and a set of snowmen like Russian dolls on her bedside table. That was it. She could cope with that amount of decoration. That was enough Christmas.

And so she'd gone to sleep and slept like the dead until now, when Kristjan had knocked at her door and woken her.

'Come in.'

He opened the door with a smile and brought in a breakfast tray, laid it on her lap. There were scrambled eggs and toast, hot chocolate in a mug shaped like a Christmas present, a bowl of muesli with a small jug of milk, and in a small bud vase a sprig of something that looked like mistletoe.

She picked it up and raised an eyebrow at him. 'What's this for?'

'For decoration. Don't eat that. It's poisonous.' He smiled.

She smiled back and propped herself up in bed properly, preparing to tuck herself in, then realised that he was just standing at the side of her bed staring at her, dressed in a very nice, *tight* pair of dark jeans and a checked shirt.

'Are you going to watch me eat?'

He sat on the edge of the bed and pinched a

triangle of toast. 'No. I'm going to go and get my own breakfast in just a minute.'

'Right... Am I going to get breakfast in bed every morning?'

He smiled. 'Would that persuade you to stay?'

'I'm already staying.'

'I meant after.'

She took a sip of the hot chocolate. It was perfect. 'It will take more than a breakfast tray to get me to uproot everything.'

'Ah... Okay. And just what exactly *is* "everything"? Just so I know what I'm in competition with?'

She faltered before she responded. It wasn't as if she could say *family*. Her adoptive mother was dead. And her adoptive father... Well, he'd left years ago. When it had all got too much for him. He'd been a coward. He'd not been able to stay and watch the progression of the disease that had been slowly killing his wife and had instead left *her* to do so.

Life had been cruel to Merry. Her real mother had abandoned her and her adopted one had faded, day by day, until death had enveloped her with its icy grip and taken even that relationship away from her. It had made her think that maybe she was destined always to be alone?

That was why this was such a shock. The fact that Kristjan wanted to be involved with her baby. Was trying to keep her here. There wasn't much left for her at home any more, except bad memories. But...

'My friends. My *job*...'

He nodded and stood up again, swallowing the last of the toast he'd pinched, licking his fingertips to get at the melted butter, and she felt her loins curl with lust at the image. She knew what that tongue could do, applied to all the right places...

'All right. Enjoy your breakfast. We need to be at work in one hour.'

'Okay.'

He headed out of the bedroom.

'Kristjan?'

He turned. 'Yes?'

'Thank you. For breakfast in bed. It was very kind of you.'

He smiled at her and nodded. 'You're very welcome, Merry.' And then he was gone.

She heard his big form going down the stairs

and she couldn't help but think, as she had last night, about what she'd agreed to. Staying here until after Christmas. Letting him try to show her that it might be worthwhile for her to stay here.

She didn't want to tell him that her home, back in Brighton, was a tiny flat with just a few pieces of furniture. A place she barely ever stayed at, because she worked so much. Or that her downstairs neighbour thought nothing of playing rock music into the early hours of the morning. Or that she'd lost most of her friends when she'd moved there to get away from her life with Mark.

Yes, she had her job—but she could do that anywhere. Her colleagues were great, but she never socialised with them. Unless you counted the Christmas party, and she'd never really enjoyed that—watching people pair up with people they wouldn't normally look at, just because the Christmas spirit had got into them.

And now Kristjan wanted to try and give *her* some Christmas spirit. By showing her the joys of living in Snowy Peak.

He wanted to be part of this baby's life—

which was something of a shock. A small part of her was pleased that he cared, but another part was terrified.

What if he was like her adoptive father? What if he left when the going got difficult? If it all got too hard?

Babies were hard work. It wasn't all cute pictures on social media showing sleeping babies inside giant flowers. It was explosive diarrhoea and spit-up, and crying into the long hours of the night.

Heck, what if *she* couldn't do it? Her own mother had failed and walked away. What was there to say that *she* would make a good mother? It was hardly in her genes, was it?

The fear of the future, of the unknown, cast a long, dark shadow...

CHAPTER FIVE

'ARE YOU READY? We need to get going.'

Merry was putting on her borrowed snow boots for the walk from Kristjan's house to the hospital. It had taken them a good twenty-minutes to get there last night in the thick snow, and she'd been amazed at the sight of the starry sky. It looked different here than it did in England—clearer...the stars brighter.

Walking behind the tall hulk that was Kristjan, she had struggled to keep up with him. He was used to this snow. She wasn't. A couple of times he'd had to stop to let her catch up, and at one point he'd had to take her hand and help her through a particularly deep patch of ice-white snow.

'Nearly ready. I just need my coat.'

'Wrap up warm—we're not going straight to the hospital.'

He pulled a thick knitted beanie hat onto his

head and opened the door as she zipped up the coat he'd lent her.

'We're not?'

'No. We've been called out to an emergency.'

'Oh!'

She thought about that. An emergency? With the roads all blocked? How would they get there?

'What are you like with dogs?'

She raised her eyebrows. 'Dogs?'

He smiled enigmatically and went outside. Merry followed and a pack of nine dogs, all tethered to one another, came galloping around the end of the street, pulling a fur-lined sled behind it.

Merry stood watching in awe. The dogs were the kind of huskies that she'd seen on television once, in a mix of colours—grey, white, brown. The front dog, leading, was solid black and looked like a wolf.

'You've got to be kidding me?'

Kristjan grinned at her. 'I couldn't get any flying reindeer. Too short notice.'

She watched as Kristjan took control of the reins from the driver who had just stepped off.

'This is Henrik. He owns the pack.'

She looked at the dogs' owner, wondering what type of person had a pack of dogs at his beck and call?

'Are you coming?'

She could easily have just stood there, gawping at the dogs for ages, but she knew she had to get a grip. Somewhere there was a child, hurt or sick, and with every second she stood there, being amazed, that child suffered a little bit more.

She clambered onto the sled under the furs and found her feet touching boxes and packs. Lifting the furs, she saw that the sled was loaded with medical equipment.

'So, you always have this thing ready to go?'

Kristjan grinned and nodded. *'Yah!'* he yelled, and cracked the reins.

The dogs began to run and Merry gasped in delight as she was pulled down the centre of the street by the team of dogs. Powdery snow was spraying into her face, but it didn't matter. This was exhilarating!

They raced past shops and homes, all decorated for Christmas. She saw fairy lights and Christmas trees everywhere. On one corner there was a giant snowman, and further down someone who clearly had a bit more skill in sculpting snow had made a snow castle worthy of a princess!

Soon the dogs had pulled them out of town and towards Wonderland, where all those tourists took their kids to meet Father Christmas and enjoy the Christmassy village. They passed through an arch made entirely out of reindeers' antlers and down what looked like it could have been a road before the snow hit.

Suddenly the dogs turned—guided by Kristjan, no doubt—and they went off-road, through a huge pile of snow that sprayed her face with more cold powder, and then moved onwards towards the dark pine trees and forest beyond.

Merry could barely breathe. This was unlike anything she had ever experienced! She'd thought it would be a bumpy ride, but it wasn't as bad as she'd expected, and she found she had to stifle the need to scream in delight and yell at Kristjan to go faster.

The bells on the dogs' reins jingled as they ran and now, up ahead, she could see a small campsite, where a fire was crackling away, sending a plume of smoke up and into the dark sky.

Of course, she thought. *They won't get day-light here until much later.*

Behind her, Kristjan must have pulled on the reins to make the dogs halt, as their run slowly became a trot, before they stilled, panting hot breaths into the icy air.

'You okay?' Kristjan stepped off the back of the sled and held out a gloved hand for her to get out.

'I'm good!'

She wanted to say more. To say that she'd found the experience on the sled exhilarating! But she knew they were here to work, and he would appreciate that even more.

'What are we here for?'

'Kid with a suspected broken leg.' He looked around him and saw a guy clambering out of one of the far tents and begin beckoning them. 'Grab the kit.'

Merry nodded and threw back the furs, grabbing the incident bag. She passed it to Kristjan, who slung it easily over his shoulder.

'Can you bring the Entonox?'

She picked up a smaller blue bag and tramped with him through the knee-high snow towards the man standing outside the tent.

'Egill?' asked Kristjan.

The man nodded. *'Já. Sonur minn er inni.'*

Egill held the tent flaps open for them both to enter, and Merry ducked her head and went in. The inside of the tent was warmer than she'd expected, and they both hurried over to the small boy who lay on the floor, on top of a couple of sleeping bags, with one leg raised on a pillow.

'Hey, there, little man. I'm Dr Gunnarsson, but you can call me Kristjan, and this here is Dr Merry Bell. She's English. You speak English?'

The boy nodded. 'A little.'

Merry knelt down beside the boy and smiled at him. 'What's your name?'

He looked shyly up at her. 'Arnar.'

'Can you tell us what happened, Arnar?' asked Kristjan, taking off his woollen gloves and putting on some medical ones.

'I try to climb tree.'

'And you fell?'

Arnar nodded his head and winced slightly.

Merry looked down at his legs, still clad in a thick snowsuit. 'How high were you in the tree?'

'The top.'

Merry turned to look at the boy's father. 'How high was that?'

'I guess about eight feet? I was in the tent making breakfast. I thought he was just playing. He'd been chasing rabbits.'

'Okay. Well, we're going to have to take a look at that leg, Arnar.'

The boy nodded.

'And we're going to have to cut open your suit, because we don't want to move your leg if we don't have to.'

Kristjan unzipped the medical bag and found the scissors and began gently cutting the suit from the ankle upwards. Whilst he did that, Merry continued with her questioning.

'Did you hit your head, Arnar?' She pointed at his skull.

'No.'

'You're sure? Can I take a look?'

She began to feel around the boy's skull, checking that there were no signs of fluid leaking from his ears or nose and constantly asking him questions as she worked, to check his level of consciousness and response. There were no visible wounds to his head or neck…

nothing she could palpate amongst the bones. She gently checked his clavicles, and then both arms and his chest.

She turned to his father. 'Have you given him any painkillers?'

'We gave him some *ibúfen*.'

She frowned. 'Is that ibuprofen?'

Kristjan nodded. 'Look at this. Visible malformation of the lower leg towards the ankle. We need to splint him. Arnar? Merry is going to give you some medicine to breathe in. It's called Entonox and it's a painkiller, okay? It may make you feel a little woozy...*svimandi*... and it might give you a dry mouth, but that's okay. It will help, all right?'

'Okay.'

She unzipped the bag, attached a new mouthpiece to the tubing and passed it to Arnar. 'Okay, you breathe in and out with this...' Kristjan translated quietly as she spoke '...without removing your mouth from the mouthpiece. It's got a special two-way filter, so you just keep breathing...nice and steady. Can you hold this for me?'

She passed the child the Entonox, so he could hold it himself—that way she could help Kristjan with applying the splint and keep Arnar calm when his leg was moved.

'Now, we're going to move your leg to apply the splint and make sure you have good blood flow.' She smiled at the boy and then turned to look at Kristjan. 'Good dorsalis pulse?' she whispered.

He nodded, whispering back, 'Yes, but we still need to adjust the break by pulling on his foot.'

'Okay.' She turned back to Arnar. 'I'm going to hold your other hand, and I want you to try and relax, Arnar—okay? Keep breathing for me…that's it. Nice and deep. In and out.' She looked up at the boy's father. 'Egill, can you talk to him? About anything, really. Keep his mind off the adjustment.'

Egill nodded and knelt down by his son and began chatting in Icelandic.

Merry couldn't understand a word, but she helped Kristjan lay an inflatable splint under Arnar's leg and then watched as he took hold of the boy's foot and quickly, expertly, pulled it back into place.

Arnar groaned.

'Keep breathing in the gas!' she told him.

'You're doing great, Arnar!' said Kristjan. 'I'm just fastening the splint now, and then you're going to get a ride on a dog sled. Ever been on one of those?'

Arnar removed the mouthpiece and nodded. 'My dad has one.'

'They're great fun, aren't they? Merry took her first ride on one today, to get here and see you!'

The boy smiled at Merry, and then Kristjan scooped him up easily and carried him out to the sled.

The dogs lay in the snow, completely oblivious to the cold, their hot breath freezing in the air around them.

Merry helped wrap Arnar in furs and then fastened him to the sled with a couple of safety belts. She got in alongside him. 'Ready?'

He nodded, smiling, happy on the Entonox.

Kristjan clambered onto the back of the sled and called out to Egill. 'We'll be at the children's hospital in Snowy Peak. You know it?'

The father nodded. 'I'll follow. I have skis.'

'Okay.'

Kristjan cracked the reins and shouted to

the dogs to get going and they all clambered to their feet and began to trot.

Kristjan guided the sled out of the trees towards Wonderland, in the direction of Snowy Peak. Merry found herself marvelling at the way people got around in Iceland without even thinking about it.

In England, snow had people hiding away indoors, moaning about the icy roads, being stranded on motorways, or complaining about the disgusting slush as everything melted away afterwards, saying that everything seemed to slow down or stop because of snow. But here they just adapted. The weather was expected to be like this, and they thought nothing of it. They had dogs, or sleds, or skis. Snow was a way of life here. Blocked roads? They didn't matter. They'd find another way. In Britain, if a road was blocked, someone would have to complain to the council before anything got done.

She took hold of Arnar's hand under the furs as they raced back to the hospital with their patient. She hoped he wouldn't need an operation. The bone hadn't broken the skin, but they had no real idea of how bad the break was or whether he'd need plates or pins.

He kept on taking the occasional suck of Entonox, especially if they bounced about as they went over some of the shallower bits of snow where there was less padding on the road.

They passed under the antler arch and she noticed a couple of people waving at them as they flew by. She and Arnar waved back, smiling, as they headed towards the busier roads of Snowy Peak. They passed a snow plough, with bells jingling on the front, and the driver waved at Arnar and tooted his horn in greeting.

Arnar looked up at her and smiled, and she couldn't help but smile back. The people here seemed so friendly! Maybe it was just the time of year, and people had a tendency to be nicer during the festive season, or perhaps that was just how they were. A small community who looked out for one another because they all knew how difficult life could be sometimes?

Kristjan wanted her to stay here. At least to consider it anyway. So he could see his child. So he could be a father.

She hadn't expected even to be thinking

about this. Changing everything. Was it possible? Or was she just looking at everything with rose-tinted specs because she wanted to believe?

They slowed down as they got closer to the hospital doors and Merry recognised Henrik, who had brought them the dog sled in the first place, coming out of the hospital, pushing an empty wheelchair with a leg rest. He was all wrapped up in a thick sheepskin coat.

He waved a greeting and the dogs barked at him in happy recognition.

'Here you go, Henrik! Back in one piece.'

'Thank you. How's the boy?'

'Suspected tib and fib fracture. We need to get him to X-Ray.'

'I've got the chair ready.'

'Good man. I never introduced you properly earlier... Henrik? This is Dr Merry Bell.'

She clambered down from the sled to shake his hand. 'Hello.'

He smiled. 'I'm the guy they come to when they want to attend a rapid response event. Mostly the dogs take tourists out, but in bad weather I keep them at my kennels for emergencies.'

Behind them Kristjan was lifting Arnar easily from the sled into the chair.

'Your dogs are wonderful. Very strong. Very quick.'

'The best hounds in Snowy Peak by far. The secret is to feed them reindeer.'

'*Reindeer?*' Merry felt her stomach churn at the thought.

'Because then they fly!' He boomed a laugh and clambered onto the sled, urging the dogs into a slow trot.

She turned to look at Kristjan and Arnar, who were both laughing at Henrik's joke. She pursed her lips, as if she was offended, but couldn't keep a straight face and laughed too.

'I guess I walked right into that one, huh?'

'You certainly did,' said Kristjan. 'Now, then, Arnar—shall we get you registered and then take some pictures of your leg?'

Arnar pointed towards the doors. 'Let's go!'

Merry followed them inside.

'Look at that. He's fractured both the tibula and fibula shafts.' Kristjan pointed at the X-ray on the screen of the computer.

Merry sighed beside him. 'It's a comminuted fracture. He'll need surgery.'

A comminuted break meant that the bone had broken into more than two fragments.

'I'll get him referred to the surgeons. They'll need to come down and talk to Arnar's father.'

'Poor kid. He was just out there trying to have some fun.'

She was leaning over his shoulder to see the screen and he couldn't help but breathe in her scent. She smelt good enough to eat and it was highly distracting...

The time they'd spent together on that short trip to collect Arnar had been enlightening. He'd not been sure how she would react to the dog sled, but she'd seemed to enjoy every minute. At one point he'd looked down on her from his vantage point as he'd steered it and had seen a huge smile on her face, and he'd smiled himself at her pleasure.

It was important to him that she enjoyed her time here if he was to have any contact with his child, and he'd lain awake in bed last night, very much aware that she was in his guest bedroom, trying to figure out how he felt about having her there. Because if he had the baby in his life then she would be in his life too, and that would mean forming a commitment to someone else—something he had avoided at all costs.

Now it was unavoidable, and how did he feel about that? Everything had changed since yesterday. He'd expected a normal day at work and now this… A relationship was the last thing he wanted, and yet in the space of a few hours he'd gone from a confirmed bachelor to a prospective father, practically living with the mother of his child!

He certainly liked having Merry close. She stirred his blood like no other woman had ever done. He'd counted himself lucky that she lived in a whole other country, so he wouldn't be tempted to follow up how he'd felt about her in Hawaii, but… Even now he could easily turn her to face him and guide her lips to his—but they were at work, and there were boundaries, and…

Was it worth breaking all his rules for this woman? He had to remember what was important here. He was doing this for his *child*. Not for her. And, although she was staying in his home for now, she wouldn't always be. It was temporary. A means to an end, right now. He had to think of the bigger picture.

If only she wasn't so damned desirable!

With a growl, he pushed himself away from the screen, knowing he needed to get some space. Some perspective. She was getting under his skin and he didn't like it. He wasn't used to it.

'I'll go tell the father.'

'Okay.'

He stalked away, trying to work out why he felt so damned irritable all of a sudden. Was it because she had changed his entire future by turning up here? Because the news of her pregnancy had derailed everything he'd thought important? Perhaps he'd been a fool to think he could get through life without forming any meaningful attachments? But it had worked so far, and he'd thought he was doing fine—until she'd told him that she was expecting their baby, and then he'd jumped tracks. Just like that. The idea that she was carrying his daughter, or his son, had suddenly become the most important thing in his world, and he didn't want to let it go.

I want to be the best father there is. My child

deserves it. I lost my parents. I can't let my son or daughter lose their father.

So he couldn't let her go, could he? And the inclement weather was doing him a huge favour! All he had to do now was work out how he was going to adapt to having Merry in his life. His body yearned for her in ways he couldn't imagine. His desire to touch her was incredibly strong...to absorb himself in her the way he had in Hawaii...

Perhaps if they slept together one more time he'd be able to get her out of his system?

Or was that the most ridiculous thought he'd ever had?

What if it worked the other way and it left him craving more? Because that was how he felt right now. Like an addict—wanting more. She was his drug. His oxygen...

After he'd spoken to Egill, Arnar's father, he left him in the capable hands of the paediatric surgeons and went to make himself a coffee. As he passed the ward he saw a male colleague talking to Merry, saw her laugh out loud at some sort of joke. He tried not to feel anything about that and headed up to the staffroom.

It was nothing. Just colleagues chatting.

They were getting to know one another, that was all. She was fitting in at her temporary place of work. It was a normal thing to do. Making friends. But he hadn't known that Jóhann could even speak English!

As he sat with his cup of coffee he couldn't help but think about how *he* wanted to be the one to make her laugh, and that thought—that acknowledgement of his feelings—made him frown to himself and wonder just what the heck was going on in his head?

Because it wasn't normal.

Not for him.

He didn't care about that sort of thing.

He didn't care about having relationships.

Right?

'You cooked supper?'

Kristjan closed the front door behind him, stamping his feet on the mat to get rid of the excess snow, and then went over into the kitchen, where Merry stood, stirring a pot.

'Well, you made breakfast—it seemed only fair.'

'What is it?'

'Homemade minestrone soup and bread rolls that I made myself.'

She lifted a clean tea towel off the tray of rolls that were gently cooling on a rack, expecting to see him smile—only he didn't. Had she overstepped?

'I hope you don't mind. But you've been good enough to give me a place to stay—the least I can do is help out…especially since you won't let me pay you for board and lodging.'

He nodded, walking away from her, and pinched a satsuma from the fruit bowl and peeled it, popping chunks of it into his mouth. 'It's fine.'

'Really? You don't sound fine.'

'I am. It's just…an adjustment, that's all.'

She understood. 'Having someone live with you?' she asked.

He said nothing, just kept eating his satsuma.

'I get it. I do. If it's too much and you want me to go to the B&B I can do that. I'll phone them later—after we've eaten.'

Considering she'd been shocked at his offer for her to stay with him, she now felt sad at the idea of moving out. Kristjan had such a lovely home—even if it did look like Santa's grotto. It was warm and comfortable and spacious. With huge comfy sofas, squishy pillows and blankets, roaring log fires. And it was the perfect situation for them to get to know each other a bit more.

She had no doubt that the B&B would struggle to be as comfortable as this place. But she would move if Kristjan was having second thoughts about inviting her into his home.

'No. Don't do that. Stay. Please.'

'Are you sure?'

He nodded. 'Yes.' He dropped the satsuma peel into the kitchen bin and then washed his hands, drying them on a towel patterned with snowmen.

She couldn't help but smile. Kristjan really loved Christmas, didn't he? He'd gone all out, putting to shame all those houses she'd seen at home, festooned in lights and outdoor decorations. They were nothing compared to Snowy Peak. They were nothing compared to Kristjan.

She tried her hardest not to stare at him, but it was difficult. She had been intimate with this man. He had seen her naked. Had stroked every inch of her skin. And she, in turn, knew every pore of his body. The feel of it. His solidity. His strength. How it felt to have him lie alongside her, to feel his arms wrapped around her body, to have his lips caressing her most intimate places...

Sometimes when she was with him it was all she could think of. And now she stood in the heart of his home, making dinner, filling the house with the aroma of delicious delights, and all she could think of was forgetting the soup, turning off the hob and stripping him naked right there and then.

But she knew she couldn't. It would be an impulsive mistake and she'd learned before that impulsiveness only got her into trouble.

'Why don't you take a seat and I'll serve this up?'

'Okay.'

She turned away from him as he sat down at the table, knowing she couldn't look at him a second more—because if she continued to look at him she wasn't sure she'd be able to control her impulses. Her desire for him went to her very core, and she knew she couldn't rely on desire, or lust, or anything like that. It was a fantasy. It wasn't real. Once the impulse went away you were left with nothing but a big mistake, and her child's future was not something she was willing to gamble with.

She'd already set the table—after rummaging through his cupboards to find crockery that didn't have a Christmas pattern on it. But it seemed Kristjan had swapped everything for the festive season, because all his plates and bowls and dishes were white with silver snowflakes painted on them, and she'd resigned herself to accepting the fact that if she was to stay here she'd have to get used to Christmas again. Because she sure as hell wasn't going to be able to avoid it!

Using a ladle, she scooped up the soup and filled two bowls to the top. She placed one in front of Kristjan and one in front of herself, then brought a small basket of her freshly made rolls over to the table.

'I hope you like soup?'

'I do. But I haven't had homemade soup for a long time.' He took a sip and gave a pleasantly surprised smile. 'This is delicious! How did you learn how to make it?'

'The internet!'

Kristjan had a healthy appetite. He polished

off his first bowl and had a second. As well as two more bread rolls. She watched him eat it all with a warm, self-satisfied smile.

'I hope you've got room for dessert?'

He raised an eyebrow and looked at her.

She blushed and hurriedly got up from the table. 'Not that kind. The kind you eat.'

'That's what I was thinking of.'

She tried not to let him see how flustered she was and busied herself in the kitchen, putting their bowls into the dishwasher.

'It's not homemade. I bought it on the way home.'

'What is it?'

'Erm… I'm not sure how to pronounce it, but I saw it in a bakery. It's an oaty pastry with a fruity jam in latticework.' She pulled it from the fridge to show him.

'Ah. *Hjónabandsæla.*'

She frowned. 'What does that mean?'

'Wedded bliss.'

'You're kidding?'

'No.'

'Oh.'

She brought the pie to the table and sliced it,

serving him a piece on a snowflake plate. Perhaps she should change the subject?

'Tell me why you love Christmas so much. It's a time for families and relationships, and you've told me you're not the relationship type.'

'You're right. I'm not.'

'So…why?'

'My parents loved it. They passed that love on to me, and after they died it just seemed the right thing to do. Go mad with the décor. It makes me feel close to them. And it's a time for miracles, isn't it? People are happier at Christmas, and I like people to be happy.'

'I'm sorry about your parents.' She remembered what he'd told her that night in Hawaii. 'It was a car crash, wasn't it?'

'On the very mountain pass that you came up on, during a storm. You can see why I wasn't thrilled about you going out in it again.'

She nodded. No wonder he was tied to this place. Memories abounded for him. Whereas she'd always moved about. Her adoptive mother had gone from place to place, looking for the best medical help, although it had never been enough to stop what was happening to her.

'Tell me why *you* hate Christmas,' he said. 'Don't think I don't see you sneering at my decorations.' He smiled.

She gave a small laugh. 'I made the biggest mistake of my life one Christmas, and every year when it comes around it reminds me of that.'

'Will you tell me what happened, or do I have to guess?'

Merry sighed. 'I got married on Christmas Eve—really, really young, when I ought to have known better. I allowed myself to get swept up in the romance of an older man and the magic of the season and it all went wrong.'

'You're divorced?' He sounded surprised.

'I am.'

'Is this husband the man you mentioned earlier?'

She nodded. 'Yes. Mark. My biggest mistake. My biggest regret.'

'What happened?'

He seemed genuinely interested, and she figured there was no harm in telling him. Why not tell him? He'd opened up his home to her—it was only fair she opened up in return. They were going to be in each other's lives for a long time.

'I met Mark at a club that I'd conned my way into, after saying I was much older than I was.'

'How old were you?'

'Eighteen. But you had to be twenty-one to get in. It was really claustrophobic in there. You couldn't move for people. It was dark, there were strobing lights, but I caught the eye of a bartender, who was doing all this amazing stuff with cocktails. Did you ever see that film where they throw everything about and mix drinks?'

Kristjan nodded.

'That was Mark. Only much cooler because I was seeing it in person. The second our eyes met I thought he seemed to be putting on a display just for me. He was slick and charming, wise and funny. We got talking. Then talking became flirting, and before I knew what was happening we were totally in lust and couldn't keep our hands off one another. He persuaded me to elope with him to Gretna Green and we got married on Christmas Eve.'

She remembered what that had felt like—the excitement, the thrill that she'd found someone who saw the real her and wanted to be with her. She'd been so used to being abandoned that finding someone who wanted to commit to her and love her had been intoxicating.

Kristjan sat listening, his face unreadable. 'And then what?'

She laughed cynically. 'We were filled with the joy of the festive season! Life was joyous! Good will to all men! We came back from an amazing honeymoon—a weekend in New York that we'd got at a bargain price through someone Mark knew—and then reality hit hard. The bubble burst. He returned to work, I returned to medical school, and Mark became a different person.'

'How so?'

How much should she tell him? Did he need to know all her sordid secrets? Did he need to hear about how ashamed Mark had made her feel? How weak and pathetic? How he'd hated the time she'd spent away from him, surrounded by handsome younger guys?

'He became insanely jealous. Possessive. I couldn't go anywhere without him wanting to know where I was going, who I was going to speak to and whether the clothes I was wearing were appropriate. He tried to tell me what to wear, how to clean the flat, that my make-up wasn't necessary. He became this angry person I didn't recognise and I was afraid of him.'

She didn't mention the endless hours she'd spent stroking his ego to try and make him feel better. How she'd tell him over and over again how much she loved him to try and put the smile back on his face and get back the old Mark she'd first known. How puzzled she'd been, having not expected love to be this hard and this complicated.

'Was he violent?'

'Not to begin with. It started small. An accident at first, or so he claimed, and of course he was dreadfully sorry afterwards. I'd driven him so mad with jealousy, he couldn't help it, he said. If only I'd done this or done that… Basically, his anger was all my fault.'

That first time she'd been in so much shock she'd utterly convinced herself that his grovelling apology was real. That it truly had been a mistake and that maybe, just maybe, she *had* been the one at fault, driving him to this state.

Before knowing Mark she'd been absolutely certain of what she thought was acceptable in a relationship and what wasn't, and she'd felt sure that if a man ever hit her she would leave immediately. But when it had actually happened… It had been more complicated. And she'd thought she still loved him.

She'd been in turmoil, needing to speak to someone—anyone—and she'd finally confided in a friend. She had persuaded her it was dangerous to stay with Mark and, realising that her marriage, her dream, had failed, she'd felt devastated.

'Didn't you try to leave?'

'I *tried*. A fellow medical student offered me her floor to sleep on. But he tracked me down.'

She paused, thinking about that night when he'd found her. What he'd done to her. She'd been so scared, and when he'd threatened to kill himself if she didn't go back with him she'd been afraid of having his death on her conscience. So she'd gone back with him, thinking that this time it would be okay… they'd work on everything. He loved her!

But all he'd wanted was to get her on her own. To get his revenge for the humiliation she had laid upon him by leaving.

'He punished me for leaving, made me

scared to make a second attempt. But the next day when he went to work I took my chance and went to the police. They got me a place at a women's refuge until I could get back on my feet again. So there you have it. I'm not a fan of Christmas and not a big fan of making rash decisions.'

'I'm sorry you got hurt.'

She shrugged. 'It wasn't your fault, was it?'

'Nor was it yours.'

Merry stared back at him, a little disconcerted. She'd always thought it *was* her fault. For Kristjan to say it wasn't, was... Well, she didn't know *what* to think.

He was surprising. This man she'd met in Hawaii, the man with whom she'd thought it would be fun to pass a hot night with, most definitely had more depth to him that she had first assumed. He wasn't just a plaything, a feast for her eyes and her senses. He was clever and kind and—dared she say it?—openhearted.

Dr Kristjan Gunnarsson was most definitely turning out to be a surprise.

CHAPTER SIX

HE COULDN'T GET it out of his head. All that Merry had shared with him that night over dinner. Once again he lay in his bed, stewing over his emotions and feelings, trying to sort them and understand them.

That she had been treated so badly by a man... It was the kind of thing that made his blood boil and made him feel ashamed to be part of the same species.

He was glad she was out of it. He was glad that she had gone to the police. She must have felt so scared. So alone. He would never let anything like that happen to her again. Not if he was around—which he hoped to be. If she stayed...

But it was these protective feelings now being created in him that disturbed him. Those and the fact that she lay in bed in the room next to his with his baby in her belly.

He'd not expected to feel this way. Not expected to feel so strongly.

Unable to sleep, he threw off the thick blankets, pulled on a white tee shirt and went to get a drink of water from the kitchen. He didn't want to disturb her, so he tried his best to be quiet, but he knew he was wide awake and wouldn't sleep yet, so he started doing a bit of a workout, hoping exercise and exhaustion would help him get a few hours' rest before tomorrow.

He worked his way through a few repetitions of sit-ups, plank side-dips and press-ups before starting a set of burpees. Then he got his weights out from behind the couch and began doing some arm curls.

It felt good to work off his frustration and his anger and finally, when he felt spent, he downed the rest of his water and turned to head back to his bedroom.

Merry stood watching him.

He hadn't heard her come out of her room.

'Sorry. Did I wake you?'

She shook her head. 'No, I was thirsty and I…er…didn't want to throw you off your rhythm.'

He shrugged. 'I couldn't sleep. What would you like? Water? Hot milk? I could do you some cocoa? Or a hot chocolate?'

'I don't feel thirsty any more.'

Really? Then why was she looking at him like that? With desire in her eyes and a gentle flush in her cheeks, her dark honeyed eyes all wide and alluring?

It was a temptation, her looking at him that way. He could feel the tension in the room. Was aware how few clothes either of them were wearing. They could be naked in seconds. He could show her all the delights he had dreamt of showing her since she'd started staying in his house.

He'd yearned for this woman after Hawaii, and been so thankful there was a huge body of water between them.

Now there wasn't.

But doing something about it would constitute—what?

They were already working together and almost living together. She was pregnant with his child. If he started to have sex with her too…

He didn't want her to misread the signals.

Yes, he wanted her. He could feel his arousal now, just standing looking at her, and, boy, did he want to submit to his needs and desires. But it wouldn't just be sex, would it? Their relationship was complicated enough without them getting *involved*. He couldn't get into a physical relationship with this woman and then develop feelings for her, because then she would mean something special and what if he lost her?

Was he mistaking convenience for desire? And how could he forget what she'd told him? She'd admitted she'd fallen in lust with a man before and it had all gone wrong for her. And if this wasn't lust they were both feeling then he was the Pope.

He was trying to convince her to stay here permanently so he could see his child—so he could be a father every day and not just on holidays and birthdays. Did he really want to screw this up? Because if he got into a relationship with Merry and it failed then he would only have himself to blame when she went running back to England.

He walked over to her…hesitated, fighting his inner turmoil.

Don't kiss her. Don't kiss her. Don't kiss her.

'Goodnight, Merry. Sleep well.'

And with a great amount of determination and anguish he side-stepped her and went into his own bedroom, closing the door softly behind him.

Inside his room, he let out a huge breath of frustration and headed to his en-suite bathroom.

He most definitely needed a cold shower.

'Hello, I'm Dr Bell. Can you tell me what's brought you in today?'

Merry smiled at the family before her. A mum, a dad and a little girl. Kristjan had assigned a nurse to work with her and quietly translate as she talked with her patients.

'We saw our doctor this morning because Hekla had been suffering with bad tummy pains and occasional sickness.'

'Is that nausea or actual vomiting?'

'Being sick, yes. Not always. Sometimes. But it has been getting more frequent. He felt her tummy and said he could feel a lump, and then he referred us to come straight here.'

'Okay...'

Merry appraised Hekla. She was a very slim girl. Pale. Twelve years old. With lovely long, golden hair that she currently wore in plaits—one of which she was chewing the end of.

Her mother pulled it from her mouth.

'No other health worries that I should be aware of? No allergies?'

Mum shook her head. No.

'So, Hekla, can I take a look at you? Do you want to hop up onto this bed for me?'

Hekla used the footstool to get up onto the bed and sat on the edge.

'I'm going to listen to your chest first, okay?'

Merry used her stethoscope to listen to the girl's heart and lungs. They both sounded completely normal.

'And this little thing is a SATS monitor. It goes on your finger—see?' She slipped it on and pressed the button. 'This will tell me how much oxygen you're breathing in and your pulse rate, and on your other arm we'll do your blood pressure. The cuff will squeeze your arm tight, but it shouldn't hurt.'

She carried out her basic observations and happily they all came back normal.

Merry smiled at Hekla. She seemed quite

anxious, but who wouldn't be if they felt ill and had been sent to hospital?

'Can you lie down for me? I'm going to feel your tummy—is that okay?' It was always important to her, when carrying out a physical examination on a child, that she told them what she was doing and they gave her permission.

'Yes.' Hekla lay down flat.

Merry began her assessment. First she visibly looked at the shape of the abdomen, to see whether there were any skin abnormalities or distention, but it looked fine. Then she began to palpate with her fingers, pressing and feeling the child's tummy, checking for masses or crepitus, and she instantly found what the doctor had. A mass about the size of a golf ball that shouldn't be there.

It was hard to feel, as it seemed to keep disappearing, and this made Merry suspect that it was probably in the digestive tract rather than attached to the abdominal wall. She unhooked her stethoscope from around her neck and listened to Hekla's bowel. It sounded normal, but something wasn't right.

'Okay, so I think we need to do a scan, Hekla. What we'll do is send you to another room where a big machine will take a picture of your tummy for us. Just to give us a clearer idea of what's going on. I think something might be blocking your tummy. You've not swallowed anything you shouldn't have?'

The young girl shook her head.

'Okay.' She pulled down Hekla's top and addressed the parents. 'We're going to send her to CT. You can both go with her. Once we get the result we might have a better idea of what's going on.'

'Thank you.'

'No problem.'

She left the family group in the cubicle and went to the doctors' station to call the scanning department and book Hekla in. Once that was done she called Olaf Ward, the children's ward, to make sure they had a bed, as she suspected Hekla would need surgery.

As she got off the phone Kristjan arrived at the desk, looking particularly delectable in a navy suit and waistcoat that emphasised the light blue of his eyes. Instantly her body went on high alert—the way it had last night, after she'd watched him exercise, when he'd walked right up to her and for a very brief moment she had thought—*hoped*—he would kiss her.

Her sex drive was high anyway, but pregnancy was making her feel as if it was firing on all cylinders—especially with him around, giving her her own private viewing of him working out. All those muscles working in perfect co-ordination... Flexing and tensing... Moving under his skin so smoothly that she had wanted to reach out and stroke him.

It had been difficult to get to sleep afterwards! Just the thought that he lay in the next room...

She'd heard him run the shower and had lain there fighting the urge to go join him, the way she had in Hawaii. But she'd had a stern talk with herself and told herself not to be so stupid! This lust she felt was a distraction and she was not here to act on it. She was here to decide if she was going to stay in Iceland or not. She was here to assess whether she could move her entire life over here. Not to dabble in sexual games with Kristjan. Even though that would be a welcome activity. After all, she knew what he was like in bed and she knew it would not be a disaster...

But sex complicated matters, didn't it? One-night stands were fun, but they were fleeting, and there was nothing fleeting about their set-up right now. Getting into a relationship with Kristjan, even if it was just a sexual one, would just muddy the waters.

'Hey,' she said.

'Hey. How's it going? Your translator working out well for you?'

'Yes, Agnes is great. Just waiting for my patient to go to CT.'

'Ah. I've been up to check on Arnar and his leg. He's had his surgery and he's doing well. He's sitting up in bed playing computer games against one of the nurses.'

'Oh, that's good...'

Kristjan had big, wide hands. Strong. Capable. Nice clean nails. She couldn't stop looking at them. Remembering how they'd felt upon her body, how he'd cupped her breasts with them, how they'd slid so nicely down her back and over her bottom and held her against him. How was such a huge, strong man so gentle...?

'Merry? Are you okay?'

'Sorry—what?'

'I told you he should be going home today

on crutches, but you seemed to be in another world.'

She smiled, feeling her cheeks flame red at her naughty thoughts. 'I am. I'm in Iceland.'

She got up and headed back to Hekla's cubicle, so she could escort her to the scanning department. It was easier to think without Kristjan around.

She left Hekla and her parents in the capable hands of the nurses on the CT unit and then went to sit in the doctor's booth to await the images on screen.

In front of her was a big window through which she could see the nurses getting Hekla into position and comfortable, with a pillow under her knees to support her. Then they pressed a button or two and Hekla slid into the machine.

Merry looked at her computer screen, awaiting the images, and suddenly there they were, showing that Hekla had a six-centimetre mass in her duodenum, almost blocking the pyloric sphincter. No wonder the girl had pain and kept being sick.

But what was it? Was it malignant? No one

would know until they opened her up. Hekla needed surgery.

Sighing, she got up to go talk to the parents.

'A what?'

The surgeon smiled. 'A trichobezoar.'

'A hairball?'

She remembered how Hekla had been chewing on the end of her plait. Was it really that she had consumed so much hair it had built up in her gut? Was it just a habit, or something more going on?

'Okay, thanks,' she said.

'I'll go and talk to the parents in case they have any questions about the surgery.'

'All right. I'll check on Hekla when she's brought back to the ward.'

She thanked him again and headed to the staffroom. It had been a long day and her feet felt tired and she was hungry. She thought of Hekla, chewing on her hair so much it had built up and blocked her insides. Poor thing!

But there was something else bothering her right now. She was having one or two cramping pains, and in the bathroom she noticed there was a spot of blood in her underwear.

Heart pounding, she stood there wondering what to do. Was she losing this baby...

No! This can't be happening! It can't!

This baby was her first opportunity to have an actual relation by blood! A child! Someone she could adore who would love her unconditionally in return. She might have been shocked to have discovered she was pregnant, but now that she'd lived with the idea for a while she couldn't bear the idea of losing it!

'Merry? You're white as snow. Are you all right?' Kristjan stood looking at her in the bathroom doorway.

'I'm spotting.'

He frowned. 'Any pain?'

'Some.' She could feel her fear rising. Her lower jaw beginning to tremble. She just wanted someone to hold her and tell her everything would be okay.

'We need to get you a scan.'

She nodded, feeling small and hopeless.

'Everything could still be fine.' He came towards her, took her hands in his, made her look into his eyes. 'You're going to be okay.'

'You can't know that.'

'I know. But you should try to remain positive.'

'I'm scared.'

He lowered her onto one of the couches. 'Sit here for a moment. I'll arrange everything.'

One of Kristjan's sonographer colleagues fitted them in immediately. And, after the longest twenty minutes of his life, worrying and waiting, he watched Merry finally lie herself down on the bed in an ultrasound room.

Kristjan switched off the lights. Should he hold her hand? He wasn't sure what the protocol was here. Where exactly he stood in his relationship with Merry. They were friends, he thought. They got on well and they had a searing attraction to one another that was often very distracting. They even lived together for now. But were they in a relationship?

That was something as yet undefined, and he didn't like it. For a man who always knew where he stood with everyone this was unfamiliar territory. Once upon a time it would have simply confirmed to him that his stance of not getting involved with people was the right thing, because it stopped all this worrying and wondering. But he wasn't that person any more. His child was in her belly and he was trying to persuade her to stay.

But most of all…he knew she must be scared. And probably believed herself to be alone here. With that thought, he took hold of her hand.

She turned in surprise to look at him.

'We're in this together, no matter what it shows,' he whispered.

Merry smiled, clearly grateful.

'How far along are you?' Magnús asked Merry.

'Um…coming up to fourteen weeks… I had a scan just before I came out here and the baby measured twelve weeks and six days.'

'Okay.'

Magnus was quiet for a moment as he squirted gel on her belly and moved the probe over her lower abdomen, frowning at the screen for a moment before turning it so they both could see.

'We have a heartbeat. Look.'

Kristjan stared in shock at the screen. That was his baby! Heart thundering away like a runaway train! It lay in Merry's womb like a curled bean and he could see it moving its arms and legs, as if it were trying to settle into a more comfortable position.

'Oh, my God! It's okay?'

'It's absolutely fine! Sometimes you can get a little breakthrough bleeding. We don't always know why it happens, but it does.'

'So it's going to be all right?'

Merry squeezed his hand and he squeezed back.

'As long as you take things easy. Monitor the spotting. If it gets any worse you can come back. I'll just take some measurements to check baby's growth.' He smiled at Merry, then turned his smile on Kristjan. 'Who would have thought Mr Eternal Bachelor would father a child, hey?'

'Life happens, Magnús.'

'It certainly does.'

Merry gasped. 'It's moving! Jumping!'

Kristjan had no words. None he could say, anyway. At that moment of pure joy he was struck dumb, afraid to speak in case he wept, and he hadn't shed a tear since he was a small boy who had realised for the first time that he was all alone in the world.

He'd known that being a father mattered to

him, but he hadn't realised just how much until he'd found Merry in the staffroom and she'd told him she was bleeding.

He'd seen many ultrasounds before, but nothing like this. Nothing that was *personal.* This was *his* baby. *His* child. *His* creation.

His family.

He squeezed her hand tightly and kissed the back of it.

'It's a good sign that the baby is healthy,' said Magnús. 'I'm just going to check the Nuchal Fold and then I'll take the measurements.'

Kristjan watched in fascination, unable to take his eyes off the screen, not wanting to miss a moment with his child. He could feel tears welling up and he surreptitiously wiped them away, hoping no one would say anything. It was too early to know whether he was having a boy or a girl, but this was still amazing.

Magnús focused on the baby's heart and played the heartbeat audibly, so they all could hear it as it roared away. A healthy heart. A perfect heart.

'This all looks good. Baby is measuring at just over thirteen weeks.'

'That seems about right,' answered Merry.

'Can we get a picture?' Kristjan asked.

'Sure.' Magnús printed a few off and then he was done, and giving Merry some blue paper towel to wipe up the gel from her abdomen. 'All looks good here. No problems that I can see.'

'Thank you, Magnús. It was very kind of you to fit us in.'

'No problem. I'll leave you two to get yourselves sorted out. See you later.' And he left the room.

Merry looked at him with a huge smile on her face. 'I think that was the most amazing thing I have ever seen!'

He smiled, overwhelmed. 'Me too.'

'Can we do this, Kristjan? Can we be the parents this baby needs?'

He didn't need to think about that. He knew he would sacrifice his life for his child if it needed it. 'Yes, we can. If we stay together.'

She nodded to show that she'd heard him. He wasn't sure she nodded to show she agreed with his statement. He still had no idea if she would remain in Iceland. He hoped so. He needed her to.

'Have you any plans for this evening, Merry?'

'Nothing except putting my feet up. Why?'

'There's something I want to show you.'

'Okay...'

'But let's go home and get changed first.'

'Wonderland? You're taking me to Wonderland?'

Wonderland was the big tourist attraction that sat alongside Snowy Peak. The place they'd raced through on the dog sled. And now they were approaching the big reindeer antler arch on a motorised snow sled.

Kristjan had arrived in front of his house with it and had asked her to hop on and put her arms around his waist if she needed to. She'd been wary of doing that, but the second they'd begun moving she'd clutched onto him, her arms wrapped around his waist, her face pressed into his back. For a few minutes she had allowed herself to close her eyes and just relax and enjoy the moment.

It was laughable, really. She was used to getting around places on foot or by car. Here, she'd been on a dog sled and now a snow sled! And they'd passed people wearing snowshoes and even a couple on skis!

Iceland in the winter was simply another world. Or at least it was up here in the mountains. She'd thought she'd hate not having many daylight hours, but she was getting used to the darkness and all the Christmas lights, and now Kristjan was about to throw her into a place that celebrated Christmas.

'This is a very special place to me,' he said.

He parked the snow sled to one side of the street and helped her off, and she took a moment to take in her surroundings.

Every building looked like a little gingerbread cabin. Only the snow on the roofs wasn't icing and the decorations weren't sweets. There were real lights and Christmas trees and candy canes. The streets were lit with electric candles and there was real holly and mistletoe. Everyone was dressed in winter gear—woolly hats and scarves and gloves—and from hidden speakers Christmas music played. Family groups walked from cabin to cabin, looking into shops full of wintry goodness, chocolates, gingerbread…

It was Christmas overload.

She was trying her best to hate it, and show her disapproval in her face, but it was hard to do because Kristjan was standing there looking at her with a smile as the snow gently fell in fat flakes and she couldn't help but laugh.

'What?' she said.

'You know you love it really.'

'Oh, *do* I?'

'You'll be singing Christmas carols before the night is out.'

'You want to put money on that?'

He grinned. 'Sure! I'll take that bet. How much?'

'If I sing a Christmas song before the night is over I'll work the entire day tomorrow dressed as an elf.'

'Done. Only not tomorrow. Tomorrow I want you to rest at home with your feet up.'

He held out his gloved hand for her to shake and she shook it, feeling confident about their wager. She'd never sung a Christmas song in her life! She knew the words to most of them, though. How could anyone not? They were shoved down your throat from early November.

'So…where exactly are we going?'

'The Elf Foundation.'

She raised an eyebrow. It sounded kitsch, whatever it was. 'Lead the way, my dear fellow.'

Kristjan performed a mock bow and began to walk across the street. She followed him, aware that some of the shop owners waved to Kristjan when they saw him pass.

'People know you? How often do you come here?'

'All will be revealed.'

'A man of mystery, eh?'

'Everyone has their secrets.' He smiled.

He led them past a shop that sold nothing but ornaments for Christmas trees, its window filled with miniature trains, nutcracker soldiers, reindeer and all manner of novelties. Another sold only Christmas jumpers, another only books, and at this window she stopped to look in.

Kristjan looked at her. 'Do you like books?'

'Are you kidding me? I *love* books! My favourite author is Nicola Drake. Look! They have her latest! I haven't read that yet.' Merry looked at the shop door and saw that it was closed already. 'Oh, damn! I might have to come back to get that.'

'Maybe Santa will bring it.'

'Maybe.' She turned away from the window and saw his face. 'Sorry. I'm putting a downer on the evening. You want to show me something that means a lot to you.'

She had no idea what the Elf Foundation could possibly mean to him. He was a doctor. A paediatrician. A grown man! What was he doing coming to this Christmas paradise where children outnumbered adults four to one? The Elf Foundation sounded like some silly factory shop where they got kids to help make toys, or something.

They rounded a corner and went down another street as the snow silently fell. Here she could see someone had tried to build a snowman, and it struck her that she had never done that as a kid. Mostly because there just hadn't been the kind of snow in England that had allowed her to do so. She could only remember it snowing heavily on a couple of occasions, and the snow had usually disappeared after a couple of hours.

As they passed she saw that one of the sticks that had been used to make the snowman's arms had fallen off, so she stooped down to pick it up and reattach it.

'Getting into the Christmas spirit, Dr Bell?'

'No.' She smiled. 'I'm a doctor. I fix people. And this snowman needed my help.'

Kristjan laughed and steered her away from the snowman, grabbing her shoulders and positioning her in front of another cabin.

The Elf Foundation

She read the sign that was in English and Icelandic—Álfasjódurinn. There was some smaller text below it. As they got nearer it became clearer and she read it, in shock.

Founded by Dr Kristjan Gunnarsson

She turned to look at him, hoping he would give her some explanation, but he said nothing, simply smiled mysteriously and led her inside.

Warmth hit them both. Kristjan helped her off with her coat and hung it on a hook, and then she got the chance to take in just what she was seeing.

The place was mostly filled with kids, of all different ages, and just one or two adults— staff, they looked like—were helping to organise them on a stage. Some were dressed normally, others were in costume, and she guessed that they going to perform something along the lines of a nativity play.

But there was no Mary or Joseph or Wise Men here. One person looked like some kind of mountain troll, dressed in camouflage or hunting gear, and one was dressed in a furry black outfit with a hunchback.

She felt completely confused.

'Kristjan! You're here!' One of the staff came over, a big smile on her face, and greeted Kristjan, clapping him on the back.

'Of course, Gúdrun. I wouldn't miss it! Can I introduce you to Dr Merry Bell? She's an elf, too, but she only speaks English.'

Gúdrun raised her eyebrows and smiled a greeting at Merry. 'Nice to meet you. Are you here to watch the show?' she asked in English with a thick Icelandic accent.

'Er... I guess I am!'

'Okay! We have saved seats near the front, as always, Kristjan. Give us half an hour and we'll be ready!'

Gúdrun was distracted then, by one of the boys who was moving a piece of staging that looked like a mountain.

'No, no, Bjarki! Put that back!'

Merry gave a short laugh. 'What *is* going on? And why did you say I was an elf?'

Kristjan smiled. 'All will be revealed!'

'And will you also tell me why your name is on the sign outside?'

He nodded. 'Later. After you've seen the show. Now, let me get you a drink from the kitchen. Would you like something hot?'

'Chocolate, if they've got it.'

'They have. They also do a mean *kjötsúpa* here. It's lamb soup.'

She thought it was probably very nice, but she hadn't been that keen on the idea of meat in her pregnancy so far. 'Would you mind if I stuck to the hot chocolate?'

'Not at all. Wait here and I'll go get some.'

She tried to stay out of the way as the kids and the staff prepared the set pieces on the stage and arranged and rearranged the seats in front of it. She sat down on one, settling in the cushions.

Clearly this was their first night presenting this play—whatever it was about—and nerves and excitement were high.

She watched all the excited kids, wondering if their parents were coming to watch them in the play, and it brought back memories of being at school herself, knowing that whether she was a bit-part player or in the lead role, as she once had been in a school production of *Romeo and Juliet*, there would never be anyone in the audience cheering her on.

Her adoptive mother had never wanted to show up at school events, so self-conscious about the disease ravaging her body, and her adoptive father had run out on them years before, when the Motor Neurone Disease had been diagnosed. So Merry had learnt to be independent, and proud of herself, and when the audiences clapped at the end, no matter how small a part she'd played, she'd always believed they were clapping just for her.

She hoped these kids had people coming in to cheer them on. People to wait for them after the play and give them a big hug, telling them how proud they were and then saying, *Let's go home and sit by a Christmas tree and wonder about the presents underneath.*

The doors opened and adults began to file in, clearly filled with anticipation.

Kristjan found her and passed her a hot mug. 'Be careful.'

'What's under your arm?'

'This?' He placed his own drink on the floor. 'A footstool. So you can put your feet up. You're meant to be resting, remember?'

'I'm fine!'

'And we're keeping you that way. Allow me to spoil you, Merry. I don't do this for everyone.'

She smiled. 'Really? What about your patients?'

He thought for a moment. 'They're different. Now, come on. Feet up!'

She rested them on the footstool. 'You're very bossy. Is that because your name is on the door?'

'Perhaps.'

'And what play are we about to see?'

'It's the story of *Gryla, Leppaludi and the Yule Lads*.'

She frowned. 'I've never heard of that before. What's it about?'

'Wait and see.'

The lights went down and the audience became quiet as music began and the curtains were pulled open to reveal two giant puppets that looked like trolls—one female and hunchbacked and ugly, the other male, taller and equally repulsive.

The crowd *oohed* and *booed* and Merry decided these must be the bad guys.

'Leppaludi! I'm hungry! Bring me some children to eat!'

Leppaludi sat down on his haunches. 'I'm tired! Go fetch them yourself!'

Before she knew it Merry was absorbed in the play about two trolls who ate children, lived in a cave and had thirteen sons called the Yule Lads. Each of these sons was incredibly mischievous, and they stole things and harassed the local villagers close to their cave on the thirteen nights before Christmas. The parents in the village used fear of the Yule Lads to make their children behave. The first, Sheep-Cote Clod, would try to steal milk from the sheep. Stubby would steal food, another would slam doors, and another would spy through windows and steal the children's toys. Each of them was naughtier, uglier and smellier than the last.

The play was funny and scary and so much fun!

Merry was thoroughly enjoying herself, and

when the play came to an end the audience got to their feet and gave all the child actors a huge round of applause. Merry didn't know any of them, but she was proud of them for putting on such a good show, and she was so engrossed in clapping them when they came on stage to take a bow that she was startled to realise that Kristjan was walking up the steps onto the stage, clearly about to make a speech.

She listened, enraptured.

'Good evening, ladies and gentlemen, and welcome to The Elf Foundation. I'm sure we can all agree that the children tonight put on a great play—let's show them our appreciation one more time.'

Everybody cheered and clapped.

'The Elf Foundation is a very special place to me. I wanted to create a place where any disadvantaged child, or child with a chronic or terminal illness could come to enjoy Wonderland and Christmas.'

Merry held her breath.

'I lost my parents at a very young age and I was very lonely. I didn't want other children to feel isolated the way I had felt. I wanted them to feel part of something. Part of a community. Part of something special. So I built The Elf Foundation. A place for children who felt isolated like I was. A place where they could come and learn through music and movement and then show others that they're just as important as those with families, or without health problems. Every child who appeared on stage tonight has a difficult story. Some have families but can't be with them. Some were completely abandoned. Some were chronically ill. But they all have come together to give joy to others at Christmas. Just like Santa's elves. And now I hope you will join with me in giving back to these children by singing a song to them and making a donation afterwards, if you can, so that we can continue to provide a place for these children here. Thank you very much—and if you look under your chairs you should find the lyrics to the song!'

Merry could feel her heart melting. That Kristjan should do something like this! Use his pain and his tragic past to create something so worthwhile! What a wonderfully kind and compassionate thing to do!

She reached under her seat and found the lyric sheet. In the corner, someone began playing a piano, and before she knew it, she was singing 'Winter Wonderland'.

It was only when they got to the chorus that Kristjan met her eye and winked at her, and she felt her heart pound, her feelings for him deepening as her understanding of him grew, and then realised with a start that he had won the bet. She was singing a Christmas song before the night was out. He'd done it. He'd managed to make her like Christmas.

Was it because this was so different from all the Christmases she had experienced as a child? Because here, despite the snow and the cold and the ice, there was real warmth and—dared she say it?—love and affection? Affection between children who didn't know each other. Who had come to put on this show for other people who *had* families and love, to make them smile? To make them *happy*?

It was such a selfless thing to do, and she knew she wanted to know more about Kristjan's Elf Foundation. She wanted to be involved—she wanted to be a part of this.

Could she do that if she lived in England?

Probably not.

When the song was over there were more

loud cheers and clapping, and Kristjan stepped back so that the children could take their final bow. Then he was coming back down the stairs towards her, smiling as he stood in front of her.

'Well? What did you think?'

'It was amazing, Kristjan! I loved it. That you've done this...' She became lost for words, felt tears prick her eyes, and she hated it that she was probably going to cry in front of him again. She *never* cried. She'd always seen crying as a weakness. So she struggled to get control of herself. To take a deep breath. 'I'm very impressed.'

He nodded. 'Good. And you sang!'

'Yes. I did.'

'So you'll dress as an elf the next time you're at work?'

'I will.'

Kristjan grinned. 'I can't wait to see it.'

She laughed, all the tension leaving her body as she saw the delight and mischief in his eyes. 'No. Neither can I.'

There'd been no more bleeding and the cramping had stopped. Merry had spent her day searching for causes and had discovered there were many benign reasons—a cervical polyp, heavy lifting, excessive exercise. Perhaps the plane trip and dragging her suitcase up the mountain had contributed? Or the dogsled ride? It could have been anything. But she had been reassured by the scan that everything was all right and she felt ready to get back to work.

The elf costume hung on the back of the staffroom door. Kristjan had found it for her in a cupboard next to a Santa costume—'For Christmas Day. We hand out gifts to those kids still here.'

'Do you dress up as Santa?'

'I do so proudly.' Kristjan had passed her the costume. 'Off you go. I'll take a picture when you're done. We wouldn't want to forget this.'

'Hmm…'

She took the costume now and went into a changing room. There was a green hat with a white feather that looked more akin to something Robin Hood might have worn, a green velvet tunic with big red buttons, some weird, poufy green breeches, red-and-white-striped tights, like candy canes, and green bootees with bells on.

Merry looked at her reflection in the mirror

and sighed—but she was also smiling. Was this the Christmas thaw? A few days ago she wouldn't have been caught dead wearing this stuff, but now… She was beginning to realise she didn't want to be the Grinch. She was beginning to see Christmas as something that could bring a smile to her face, and a part of her wanted that very much!

It had been exhausting to hate Christmas! And how much of that had been caused by Mark? Selfish, awful Mark.

But now she was here, in the land of Christmas, and she had Kristjan nearby, and a baby to grow, and everything seemed hopeful right now. It was a time of goodwill.

Yes, maybe some bad things had happened to her at Christmas, but that wasn't the season's fault. That didn't mean she couldn't turn it around and refuse to be a slave to her past. It was a time for new beginnings. To let go of the past and begin anew. If Kristjan could take *his* tragic past and make something positive out of it, like The Elf Foundation, then why couldn't she?

She stepped out of the changing room and saw Kristjan had a big grin on his face.

'Smile!' He lifted his mobile phone to take a picture.

Merry laughed. 'These shoes are very apt for a name like Dr Bell. The kids will think I'm making it up.' She pointed her foot to make the bells jingle.

'I think you look and sound delightful,' he replied.

'Thank you.' She walked with him to the lifts and travelled down to their ward, where Agnes, her nurse and translator, was waiting for her.

'You look…very nice.' Agnes smiled.

'I lost a bet. Now, who's first on the list today?'

She went to grab the patient file at the top of the in-tray, but Agnes got there first.

'Dr Gunnarsson said I'm not to let you work too hard today.'

Oh, did he, now? Merry turned to look at him and he shrugged.

'I'm taking care of both of you. Don't get angry.'

'I'm a grown woman. I'm quite capable of judging what I can and cannot do.'

'I know. But this isn't just about you any more, so I'd like to think I have a say.'

Irritatingly, he smiled at her before walking away.

Merry shook her head in exasperation, then smiled at Agnes, grabbed the top file from her and gazed at the details.

Ingestion of a foreign object

'Okay! Let's go!' She jingled her way to the waiting room and called out her patient's name. 'Darri Edvardsson?'

A mum, a dad and a little boy aged about five stood up.

She smiled at them. 'Hi, I'm Dr Bell. Let's see if we can sort out your problem.'

'Are you a real elf?' asked Darri.

'I am.' She smiled, thinking of the elves last night. She was one of them. One of the abandoned. And she was trying to make other people's lives better. Yes, she was an elf.

'Okay, then—it says here that you've swallowed something you shouldn't?' She was getting used to Agnes's low voice, quickly translating everything at her side, but she was beginning to wish she had the ability to speak the language herself. Maybe she should try to learn it if she stayed?

Darri's mother spoke up. 'He was playing with his toys, trying to build a crane out of those metal bits and pieces. He put a piece in his mouth as he tightened a bolt and somehow he swallowed it. I blame the cat for scaring him.'

'The cat?' Merry frowned.

'She jumped down from the window and startled him. Will he be okay? Will it pass normally?'

'Well, how big was this piece that you swallowed, Darri?'

'About this big.'

Darri showed her with his fingers, indicating a piece four, maybe five centimetres long.

'And did it have smooth edges? Was it rounded?'

'I don't know for sure,' he said.

'Well, I guess we'd better take an X-ray.'

'You don't think he'll need surgery, do you?' asked the mother.

'I'll need to see the films before I can answer that, but at the moment he seems fine.

He's not vomiting…he's not in any pain. It all looks good, so far.'

'All right…'

'I'll just go and make that referral—I won't be long.'

She jingled her way back to the doctors' desk, rang through to the X-ray department and booked Darri in. There was a wait of about half an hour, but she wasn't unduly worried. The piece of metal would probably pass straight through.

She heard Kristjan laugh from another cubicle and it made her smile. Who'd have thought that a man like him would have so much depth to his character? When she'd first met him she'd pegged him as the kind of guy you just had a quick fling with. He was fun, and sexy as hell, and she'd thought she'd never run into him again—which had been good because he hadn't seemed like the type of guy who did commitment.

And yet here he was. Opening up his home to her. Accepting her pregnancy and getting teary-eyed at the sight of their baby on the ultrasound screen. He'd opened up a place for orphaned children to go at Christmas. He cared for sick children and made them better. He was funny, kind, charismatic—and he *cared*.

I like him. I like him very much.

Which was disturbing in all manner of ways.

It wasn't meant to be happening. Her plan for a quick visit, announcing the news and then returning to England was now all skewed. And she was beginning to like certain things.

They were friends—and that was good, because they'd need to be if the future became more uncertain. She still wasn't sure what she was going to do. Stay? Or go back home?

She was going to be a mother, and her baby would have a chance to know both its parents if she stayed. Shouldn't she do what was right for her child? Shouldn't that be her top priority as a parent? You made sacrifices for your children, didn't you?

As her mother had done for her, by giving her up in the hope that she would have a better life than the one she could give her. That was what she had to believe had been the motive for her mother leaving her on a vicar's doorstep.

And her adoptive mother had done all she could to raise her before she'd got sick, and she had been devastated when Merry had become her carer at such a young age. That was why Merry had chosen to go into medicine. She'd hated feeling she couldn't do more. Couldn't understand what was truly going on.

Merry wanted to give her child what she had never had—a proper family. And by staying here in Iceland she could do that.

But…

But she'd never considered giving up her old life. There wasn't much at home, but it *was* home. *Home.*

Everything was familiar there—her job was there. They'd been good when she'd rung to say she was stuck in Iceland for a few days, and she'd felt terribly guilty about letting them down.

But which was more important? Her job? Or her child's future?

It was a no-brainer when she put it in such stark terms as that, even if in reality it would be hard.

Although she *was* beginning to love it here. The place and the people were beginning to make her consider the move as a real possibility.

And Kristjan…?

He was at the heart of the matter. He had feelings she had to take into consideration, too. He wanted to be a dad. She could see that, and that was fantastic. She'd not known what to expect from his reaction when she'd first come here.

Could she imagine walking away?

Right there and then, she wasn't sure that she could.

Her feelings for him were growing. Multiplying. And as they did so her fears grew with them.

What if this turned out to be a big mistake?

CHAPTER SEVEN

'I THOUGHT YOU might like to go out for a meal tonight.' Kristjan leaned on the doctors' desk where Merry was typing some patient notes into the computer system.

She looked up and laughed when she saw he was wearing the Santa costume—from the red hat and white beard down to the big black boots.

He had to give it to her—she had kept her word about wearing an elf costume, despite her feelings about Christmas, and she seemed to be taking it in her stride. He also had to admit that he *liked* seeing her dressed up as an elf! She looked more whimsical and beautiful than ever, and it made him smile to hear her feet making jingling noises as she walked about the department.

The patients loved it, too—especially some of the younger ones—and one or two had even asked where Santa was. Hence the costume.

He had decided to join in, and he loved how her smile now made him feel all warm on the inside.

'Dinner?'

She seemed to think about it.

'Do we get to wear our own clothes or do we have to stay in costume?'

He grinned. 'Costume would be fun, but I'll let you decide. I'm up for either.'

'Well, much as I've enjoyed being Merry the Elf today, I'm kind of looking forward to putting on something that doesn't itch so much.'

'Okay. I've got us reservations at eight o'clock at Ingrid's. It's a restaurant in town.'

'Sounds great. Thanks.'

'I thought it might give us a chance to talk about how things are going.'

Her smile faltered. 'Is there anything in particular that you want to talk about?'

'No. I just thought that usually when we get home from work we eat and then go to sleep. It might be nice to go out...have someone else cook and clean up whilst you're meant to be resting.' He smiled. 'And, you know... I think going out for dinner is what normal people do, but I'm not sure.'

She nodded, smiling. 'I've heard of the practice.'

'We might like it.'

'We might.'

He was still smiling at her, and she was smiling back, and he realised that they were so absorbed in one another that other members of staff were glancing at them with amused looks on their faces. It certainly hadn't taken long for the hospital grapevine to do its thing.

Kristjan stood up straight, adjusted his scratchy white beard and his big fake belly, and headed off to treat another patient. He felt good because she'd agreed to eat out with him. They needed to get to know one another better and time was running out. He had no idea if she was going to leave or not, and he figured if he knew more about her he might find the thing that would make her want to stay.

Who'd have thought it? The eternal bachelor was trying to make a relationship work.

The only question was…what type of relationship would it be?

What to wear?

Kristjan had said they were going out for dinner, and Merry wanted to dress up nicely for the occasion, but she didn't want him to think that she was dressing up for *him*. This wasn't a romantic date or anything. They weren't trying to *court* one another. It was like Kristjan had said. They were just going to get to know one another better.

So, what sort of dress should she wear to dinner with a friend? There wasn't much in her luggage, and she'd hardly had time to go shopping for clothes, but there was a simple black dress that she'd put in her suitcase just in case she had to meet Kristjan at a place such as a restaurant.

It will have to do.

Merry slipped into it and stared at her reflection in the bedroom mirror. It still fitted all right—her pregnancy wasn't showing too much yet, though she thought she could feel an extra rounding to her lower abdomen. Not much. But enough to notice a small change.

And my hair... I need to do something with my hair.

She pulled it back, then scrunched it up high, trying it one way, then another. In the end she just swept it up into a clip, added some small diamond stud earrings and put on some lipstick and eyeliner.

There. That's not too much. I don't look like I'm trying too hard.

She slipped into a pair of heels, sprayed her wrists with perfume without thinking about it, and stepped out into the living area to wait for Kristjan.

He was already there, dressed smartly in dark trousers and jacket and an ice-blue shirt that matched his eyes.

He took her breath away, standing there like that, looking so smart and formal, and when he smiled it went straight to her heart and it began to pound faster.

'You look beautiful, Merry.'

'This old thing? Oh, I've had it for years,' she replied, suddenly nervous.

It's not a date. It's not a date. It's not a date...

She distracted herself from his appreciative gaze by picking up her bag and coat.

'Here. I got you something.' He passed her a small parcel wrapped up in a gold paper and bow.

'For Christmas?'

'No. For now. For agreeing to stay. At least until the roads are clear.' He smiled.

'Oh… I feel bad that I haven't got you anything.'

'Just open it.'

With nervous fingers she undid the bow and carefully opened the paper to find the Nicola Drake book that she'd wanted.

'Kristjan! You shouldn't have!'

'I saw that you wanted it.'

How sweet was that? But, knowing she was in danger of being swept off her feet by this charming, sexy man, she refused to take her eyes off the book and look into Kristjan's face.

Because if she did she'd want to give him a kiss as a thank-you. And if she did that… Well, then they'd be close, pressed against each other, and she'd be inhaling his scent, feeling the solidity of his body, and her need for him might overcome all sensibility and they'd miss their dinner reservation!

'This is so kind of you. Thank you. Let me put it in my room, so I don't lose it, and then we can go.'

In her bedroom, she took a moment to rest against her bedroom wall and take a few deep breaths. What was he *doing* to her? Giving her thoughtful gifts… Dressing as Santa so she didn't feel silly being the only one in costume, even though she was the one that had lost the bet… Opening a foundation for orphaned kids…

What else would she learn about this man? There had to be a dark side. There always was. She had to remember that. She'd made rash decisions before about a man and look how *that* had turned out?

After giving herself a stern talking-to in the mirror, she pasted on a smile and headed out to join him. 'Are we ready?'

He gave a nod. 'We are. Ingrid's isn't far. But you won't be able to walk in those heels. Not in this snow.'

'I can put on the snow boots.'

He smiled. 'Those heels are nicer. We'll take the snow sled.'

She bit her lip as he helped her on with her coat, like a perfect gentleman. She was perfectly aware of him standing so close to her. She could even feel his warm breath on her bare shoulders, and it sent shivers to all those perfect places…

'Thank you.'

'Wait here. Let me bring it round from the shed.'

She waited, with butterflies in her stomach, as she heard the engine start up and the sound of the purring machine as it stopped outside the front door.

When he came in and offered her his arm he quickly grabbed a blanket from the back of the couch. 'So your legs don't get cold.'

He told her to sit side-saddle, draping the blanket over her legs, and leaned in close to tuck the blanket around her thighs. Feeling his hands on her again almost doubled her heartbeat, and she badly hoped he wouldn't notice her reaction to him. Thankfully he got onto the sled himself, wrapped her arms around his waist and held her with one hand—surely only for extra security?—as they quickly motored to the restaurant.

Ingrid's really wasn't far. It was small. Cosy. Intimate. Full of dark corners and perfect for private conversations. But it was also very aware that it was Christmas, and there were huge garlands draping from the thick wooden beams, with frosted slivers of orange and cinnamon sticks and poinsettia-red ribbons. Candlesticks gleamed. Sconces glowed. And a cascade of silver and white baubles hung from the ceiling like drops of snow.

A waiter received them and seated them in a corner booth, and Merry smiled at the table decoration. Three white tealights floating in a bowl that looked as if it had been carved from a silver birch tree.

'This is nice. Have you been here before?'

'Once or twice. We had the staff Christmas party here last year.'

'Where are you having it this year?'

'Wonderland.'

'Oh.'

'You're very welcome to come. In fact, you should make sure you do. It'll be fun.'

'Well, we'll see...'

She pretended to straighten the cutlery, though it didn't need it. The table was perfect. As was this evening. As was *he*. Which was why she was trying to find fault with it. And she felt awful for doing so.

'What would you like to drink?'

'Oh, just a fruit juice or something will be fine.'

'I'll join you.'

'You don't have to.'

'I know, but I will. I *am* driving, after all.' He signalled to the waiter. 'Could we have two apple juices, please?'

'We have apple, pear and ginger? Will that be all right?' the waiter asked.

Kristjan looked at her for confirmation and she gave a brief nod.

When the waiter had left to get their drinks, Kristjan seemed keen to get the conversation going.

'I was very impressed that you stayed dressed as an elf all day.'

'Well, I'm a woman of my word.'

'I can see that—though I'm not sure anyone else would be able to wear it as well as you did.'

She smiled. 'And *you* made a good Santa.'

'Thank you.'

'Do you think you'll make a good father?'

The question was out before she could think about what she was asking, and her cheeks flamed red with heat.

But then she thought to herself, *Well, we wanted to get to know one another a bit more.*

We might as well discuss what's going to be important...

'I hope so… Yes, I think I will be a great father. Given the opportunity.'

'You want to be involved?'

'How could I not? As soon as you told me about the baby I… And then when we saw the baby on the scan it was just…' He shook his head, clearly lost for words. 'I've never felt like that before.'

'It *was* amazing…'

She felt her heart soften at the thought of the ultrasound. To see her baby moving the way it had! Jumping, slipping, sliding, waving its arms and legs! Its little heart pounding away! A real person already! It was incredible, and it was all going on inside her body. She was creating—no, *growing* the future.

'How does it feel to know you'll soon have your very first blood relation?' he asked.

'I don't know. I veer from being amazed to incredulous to disbelieving from one moment to the next. I don't think I'll quite believe it's really there until I hold him or her in my arms.'

He nodded. 'I'll be honest with you… I never thought I wanted this until it happened, and now I just know that I want it more than any-thing.'

'I know what you mean. I'd resigned myself to being single for the rest of my life, maybe getting a cat or two, but...'

'You can still have a cat or two. We do have pets here in Iceland.'

'I'd much rather have my baby.'

She looked into his ice-blue eyes and saw exactly the same feeling mirrored back. He wanted this child as much as she did. It was a new opportunity for them both. But they needed to know how they would manage it. How it would work and who would have cus-tody.

'Do you think it's a girl or a boy?' he asked.

'I don't know.' She'd had dreams of both. 'Do you want to find out before the birth?'

'Do *you* want to?' he replied.

'I think I'd like to know. So I can plan. Dec-orate a nursery. Do all that kind of thing.'

'Agree on names?'

The waiter arrived then, with their drinks on a tray, which he served up along with their menus, before disappearing again.

Merry liked it that he didn't get in the way,

like in some places where the waiters were constantly in your face, asking questions. Did they want the wine list? Could they get them anything else? Did they like the food? She hated that.

To be fair, she didn't know if he would interrupt their meal or not, but from what she'd seen so far the staff here liked to disappear into the background and let the atmosphere and the restaurant speak for itself. Taking a sip of her drink, she nodded at how wonderful it was—sweet, with a kick of ginger that warmed the palette. 'You're thinking of traditional Icelandic names?' she asked.

'I like Icelandic names, but I'd rather pick one that we both agree on, whether it comes from my country or not.'

Damn. He was still being chivalrous. What was there not to like? Or to pick fault with? Perhaps he was too giving? Perhaps she had stumbled from one man who took and took to one who gave and gave? Was that why she was intrigued by him? Attracted to him? Because he was the polar opposite of Mark?

She would have to be careful. Very, very careful.

'I guess names can wait until we know what it is.'

'Agreed.'

They picked up their menus and she pretended to be studying the selection, but in reality she was stealing glances at him. Watching his eyes as he read the offerings, trying to see if she could detect any hint of nastiness in his features that might speak of someone with a hidden dark side. But she could see nothing but his eyes, which spoke of kindness and generosity and sex appeal. Come-to-bed eyes. Let-me-undress-you eyes. Let-me-make-you-feel-good eyes.

She'd looked so intensely into those eyes once. In Hawaii. Amazed by the man she'd been with. Kristjan. A tall Viking. With long blond hair that he wore in a plait down his back, a beard, *huge* muscles...

If it wasn't for the fact that he wore a suit and carried a cell phone she would have imagined he'd either stepped off a film set or off a longboat and mislaid his horned helmet and axe.

Perhaps it was the raw maleness of him. His outward appearance of someone who could take care of whoever he was with. Could offer protection.

Merry had never felt protected in her entire life. She'd been taken care of by her adoptive mother, but their roles had been so quickly reversed. She had never felt the way she did when she was with Kristjan.

'See anything you fancy?' he asked.

'I'm sorry—what?'

He looked at her with amusement. 'On the menu?'

'Oh, right. Sure. Erm…what do you recommend?'

'How are you with fish?'

'Good.'

'Okay. The scallops with a parsnip purée and pickled figs sound good.'

'Great.'

'Cod fillet for main? With garlic mash and champagne sauce?'

She nodded, and watched as he got the waiter's attention and gave their order. It was feeling as if they were on a date. Even though they'd both said it wasn't. But there was no way she was going to get into a relationship with this man. With *any* man, thank you very much. She couldn't afford the risk to her heart.

Did Kristjan constitute a risk? Was it wrong of her to judge him on another man's standards?

They were going to co-parent, so they were going to be involved with each other to some degree, but just how much would that be? Because if he was going to continue being chivalrous and lovely and kind and amazing, she didn't know how her poor little heart was going to end up!

Kristjan was intoxicating her.

She had butterflies in her stomach, performing a full aerobatic show.

She sipped at her juice. 'This place is nice.'

'It is. The chef is a very good friend.'

'Do you know *everybody* around here?'

'Well, when you don't have any family you make time for lots of other people.'

'And this is quite a small community?'

'Yes.'

'Do you ever find that restrictive? Knowing that everyone knows your business?'

'No. It's nice, in a way. People look out for one another here on the mountain. I know I could count on anyone to come to my rescue if I needed it.'

'You're lucky, then. I've always felt alone.'

'Is that why you got married so young, do you think? So you would have someone? To make a family?'

'Maybe… I was a bit of a daydreamer. And Mark seemed so much wiser. So distinguished. Perhaps I was looking for a father figure? I was a big romantic. I'm not now.'

'You don't make any time for romance?'

'No point. It never seems to end well. Every person I know who's in a relationship has problems and difficulties.'

'But isn't that part of human nature, though? We have problems and difficulties with our friends, too. In any type of relationship.'

'So why haven't *you* ever got involved with someone, then? What's stopped you?'

Kristjan shook his head. 'I loved my parents. When I lost them on the mountain pass it broke my heart and I swore I would never care for anyone like that ever again. Plus, I experienced a little of what you just talked about. I saw all these other people having problems, giving themselves and losing pieces of who they were just to fit into a relationship and make it work, and as I got older I decided I was *never* going to compromise who I was. I was never going to lose any pieces of myself. I was just going to be me.'

'So you've always been single? You've never been in a committed relationship?'

'No, and I never intended to be.'

'Until me.'

He smiled. 'Until you.'

The waiter arrived then, with their starters. 'Enjoy your meal,' he said.

Looking at her beautifully arranged plate of food, Merry could understand why some people took pictures of their meals. 'This looks lovely.'

But her appetite was wavering. He'd as good as told her that she was different. That she mattered. Although *was* it her? Or was it just the baby that changed everything? She hoped not. A small part of her—maybe even a large part—wanted to feel that *she* was the one making him change his beliefs. That they had something special.

The scallops were exquisite. Rich in flavour and perfect with the smooth and slightly sweet parsnip purée. And the pickled figs added the perfect sharpness to her palate.

'You don't feel like you've missed out?' she asked.

'What have I missed?'

'Camaraderie? Closeness? Intimacy?'

'I've experienced all of those.'

'Just not with the same person?'

'No.'

She sighed, not sure why this bothered her. Was it because he had no track record by which she could judge his ability to sustain a relationship? If he'd never had a committed relationship before, how could she tell how he would be? Would he get bored by the commitment after a few months, once the excitement of a new baby had worn off and the sleepless nights and the stinky nappies and the crying took its toll?

Maybe *this* was his big fault?

This was what was wrong with him?

She'd found it. His Achilles' heel.

'So you don't do commitment at all? You can see how this might bother me…what with you wanting to be an involved father and everything.'

'I've never been in a committed *romantic* relationship. But I was committed to my education and my training to be a doctor. I'm committed to my place of work. I'm committed to The Elf Foundation and have been for years. I'm committed to my friends. I can *do* commitment, Merry.' He dabbed at his mouth with his napkin. 'Can you?'

'Me?' Surely he didn't have a problem with *her* evidence of commitment? 'I got *married*!'

'Which, for very obvious reasons, didn't last. That wasn't your fault, but have you committed to anything since then? You're considering leaving your job, leaving your country...'

'That's what *you* want me to do!'

'I'm just saying...' He smiled, as if he had proved his point.

Kristjan really was the most infuriating man she had ever met. 'You've asked me to consider doing those things and I'm being open and considerate because of our situation.'

'Because at the moment you don't have a choice. The roads are impassable.'

'For *cars*. I'm sure I could use your snow sled to get down the mountain.'

His eyes darkened. 'It's too dangerous. Tell me you would never do that.'

She stared at him, then relented. 'Fine. I'd never do that.'

'Thank you. Look, I'm sorry I implied you weren't committed, but you did the same thing to me. I think we're both very tense because of what's happening. We both want to get this right and we're both committed in our own ways. Can we agree on that?'

She shrugged. 'We can't get this wrong, Kristjan. This is too important just to feel our way through and hope for the best. We have to be sure we know what we're doing.'

'I'm not sure parenting is like that. Have you ever met any parent who's *totally* in control of the situation?'

No, she hadn't. The parents she met in hospital, when their child was sick or injured, were most often out of their heads with worrying and fear. And her own adoptive mother had felt totally powerless as her disease had taken more and more away from her.

'We just have to do our best and work together—not against each other,' he said.

'And your first request is that I consider staying in Iceland permanently?'

'I would like you to consider it, yes. Can you see yourself giving up your job and your home in England?'

'I *have* thought about it.'

'And?'

'And I don't know. I really don't. I would so much love the fairy tale! The happy family. Mum and dad in one house...a happy child. The white picket fence. Maybe a dog or something. But is that realistic?'

'There's nothing wrong with wanting the fairy tale.'

'But I can't have it. Because I don't want to get involved romantically ever again and you said you don't either. Do you think we could share a house but live independent lives?' She smiled sadly. 'Do you think I'd want our child to see you bringing home random women?'

'That wouldn't happen.'

'No? Have you *seen* you? Women notice you, Kristjan. You're pretty hard to miss.'

'My focus would be on my son or daughter.'

The words he was saying were great—but they weren't realistic, were they? He was a big, virile man and he would have needs. Did he think they could live together and every so often he would go out and meet someone, hook up with them at their place before coming home to her and the baby? That would make her feel…

What? Jealous? Because that was how the idea made her feel right now. Jealous and angry and upset and…

Disturbed by the emotion, she put her knife and fork together on her plate, indicating that she was finished with her first course.

She was feeling a bit sick. 'Excuse me. I just need to use the bathroom…'

He watched her go, frustrated with the turn of their conversation. He'd hoped to clear the air of a few things, but instead they'd just muddied the waters somehow. The conversation should have remained light and breezy, but it had got serious quite quickly.

They both had desires here—and he wasn't talking sexually, though that did complicate matters too. Because no matter how much he tried to ignore the feelings he had for Merry, they kept creeping back to the surface, and the fact that she was carrying his baby was making him feel all caveman-like and protective of her, too.

He'd never felt this way about a woman before. Perhaps that was why he'd been a little prickly this evening? Biting back when she'd accused him of never being committed to anything...

Because he *was* committed! To their baby. He was committed to providing that baby with the best life, and with two parents who would love it very much!

I'll apologise when she comes back.

They could start the conversation over. Start afresh. They were friends—that would be easy enough. He didn't like how it had made him feel to upset her. It was wrong. She was the mother of his child, and if they couldn't agree right now, how would it be when the baby was here and they had to make other decisions?

When she came back to the table he stood up and watched her settle into her chair, before sitting down once more across from her. She looked a little flushed in the candlelight.

'Are you all right?'

He needed to know that she was. They'd

both had a difficult time lately, what with the scare and the whole change in circumstances for both of them. It was a lot to absorb.

She nodded, smiling.

'I'm sorry, Merry. I didn't mean to respond the way I did. I guess I'm just nervous.'

'Of the situation?'

'And of you.'

'*Me?*'

'I've never had someone important in my life since my parents, and yet here you are, carrying the most precious cargo. My child. And I know that you could leave at any minute. Get on a plane and disappear from my life.' He reached out and took her hand across the table. Squeezed it. 'You've become special and I never expected that.'

'Because of the baby?'

'Yes.'

She nodded, squeezed his hand back, then reclaimed it to pick up her glass and sip at her drink. She looked a little annoyed, not meeting his eye, and he wasn't sure why. Hadn't he just told her what she wanted to hear? He was being honest with her. As far as he could be, anyway.

The waiter came and took their plates and disappeared once again.

He looked at Merry. She was so beautiful to-night. In that little black dress that showed the smooth curve of her shoulders and bare neck. The twinkle of her earrings drawing the eye to her soft skin. Of course she always looked beautiful. Every man in this place probably thought the same thing.

He was stepping out into new and unfamiliar territory here—caring for a woman in the way he knew he was starting to care for Merry. He'd told her it was simply because of the baby, but he'd been holding something back. He didn't want her to be confused about how he felt, but how could he tell her when he couldn't admit it out loud?

I guess I'm just going to have to try to be genuine and take it day by day.

'I want you to stay, but I know that you have a home and a life elsewhere. So I'll take the reindeer by the horns and trust you completely. If you say you're considering staying here, then that's good enough for now. We'll take each day as it comes.'

She nodded. 'We will.'

* * *

The main course was fabulous, but even better was the succulent dessert of *kleinur*—a pastry similar to a doughnut, filled with rhubarb curd and dusted in icing sugar.

After the slightly sticky start to their conversation, they'd veered onto safer topics, and now it was late and time for them to go home.

Merry yawned, beginning to feel the effects of the long day on a body that was already working overtime growing another person.

'Tired?' asked Kristjan.

'Ready for bed.'

She didn't see the way his pupils dilated briefly as she was putting on her coat, but she heard him thank the maître d' and then they stepped outside into the cold, dark night.

A frost was settling, making the snow crunchy underfoot. He escorted her safely across the ice and took her hand to help her onto the sled once more for the short trip back. He went to grab the blanket and put it over her lap again, but she remembered how it had felt to have him do that before, and she was still smarting from the fact that he'd told her this was all because of the baby and not her at all.

Kristjan studied her. 'Are you okay?' he asked, concern filling his face.

Her heart was pounding, her legs like jelly. 'Yes, I'm just tired. It's been a long day.'

'Let's get you home.'

She held on to him tightly as they drove back, laying her head gently against his back as he drove at a slow speed through the snow. Merry tried to absorb what it felt like to lay herself against him, how fabulous it was, how wonderfully solid and safe he made her feel, but all it did was bring tears to her eyes that she had to wipe away surreptitiously.

At the house, he escorted her in. She peeled off her heels, wincing, and settled onto the couch.

'Remind me never to wear heels again. My ankles are the size of beachballs.'

She propped herself up and tried to focus on rotating her sore ankles, rather than on the rest of her, but all the tingling and anticipation she'd felt as she'd lain against him, and the sense that she might lose him after all, and all the wanting, was hard to ignore.

'Okay, let's have a proper look at these, shall we?' he said, and he gently lifted her feet onto his lap.

She had such dainty feet. Pixie feet. Her toenails were painted a soft rose colour. He began to massage her skin, gently manipulating her ankles with smooth, steady strokes in the hope that it would feel good. The friction caused by his hands upon her warmed his touch, and soon his massaging strokes were not just encompassing her ankles, but her feet too, and her lower legs.

It was as if he felt hypnotised, drawn to touching her. To being in contact with her. As if he couldn't let go.

He wondered what would happen if his hands moved up her leg... Past her knee... Beyond the hemline of that little black dress that so beautifully showed off her shoulders and slim arms. There was a zip down the side...it would come off in one easy movement...

He brought his thoughts back to her feet, taming them, trying to throw cold water on them, but it was impossible! Touching her, holding her, was too much for his senses to handle. His blood was racing round his body and he needed to cool down before he made a terrible mistake.

With a growl, he got up, moving her feet to the couch, and stalked away from her.

'What's wrong?' she asked.

'Nothing.'

'There's something. Talk to me.'

He turned to look at her, and all he wanted to do was take her in his arms and take her to his bed. 'The truth?'

She nodded. 'The truth.'

'If I'd kept my hands upon you I wouldn't have wanted to stop.'

Her eyes widened at his statement and her lips parted. 'Oh.'

'And I don't think that would be wise for either of us right now, would it?' he said, annoyed with his reaction to her.

'I guess not…no.'

'So, if you don't mind, I think I'll go to bed. Alone.'

'All right.'

'Do you need anything?'

'Um… I don't think so. I'd like a glass of water, though, if that's not too much trouble?'

Water. He could do that. It was practical and it was safe and it had nothing to do with caressing her body and making her his. Unless he poured that glass of ice-cold water over her naked body… Would it make her nipples peak? Strain outward, ready for his warm mouth to envelop them? Would he be able to follow the rivulets of water with his tongue? He could take a cube of ice and run it down her…

Stop it!

He gritted his teeth as he got a glass of water and took it to her room, placing it down upon her table. He tried not to imagine her in the bed. Tried not to wonder if she slept naked or not. Tried not to inhale the scent of her perfume that lingered in the room.

He headed back out and walked around the edge of the living room without looking at her, not sure if his resolve would hold if he did. 'Goodnight, Merry.'

'Goodnight, Kristjan.'

He closed the door to his bedroom and leaned back on it, wishing it had a lock, before pulling his shirt free from his trousers and slowly getting undressed.

If he had any more cold showers he'd be totally made of ice.

Kristjan woke in the early hours and, being totally unable to get back to sleep, decided to go for a swim in Snowy Peak's geothermal outdoor community pool. What he needed was to work off some of the pent-up energy that had been simmering in him since last night. It was the kind of energy that he usually worked off in a much more satisfying way, but swimming, powering through a few lengths, would have to do.

When he arrived the surface of the water was as still as a millpond, and once he was stripped to his shorts he dived in and felt the heat of the thermal waters embrace him. At that early hour there was no one else there and he had the pool to himself. As he swam, his thoughts continued to rampage in his head.

Merry. The baby. How all this was going to work itself out.

If she stayed, would she buy her own place? Would it be here, in Snowy Peak? Or would she prefer to be in Reykjavik, where there were more people? What if they had a huge falling out? Would she leave? Would she hold the threat of leaving over him for ever? And if she did leave would he follow? This community, these people, meant so much to him. His parents were buried here. He had history here. Roots.

But...

He couldn't imagine not being in his child's life.

The powerlessness, the uncertainty of it all, was immensely frustrating to him—a man who was used to being in control of everything. Perhaps that was why he'd wanted Merry last night—because he'd felt that if he could at least possess her, then she would be his? At least for a short time?

He didn't want a full-time relationship with her, did he?

Did he?

He took a deep breath and swam underwater for as long as he could, before finally breaking the surface and gasping for air, swimming in a front crawl towards the edge in powerful strokes, turning at the poolside and swimming out again, determined to exhaust himself before he returned home.

Because he liked the way she looked in the morning. The ruffled bed hair, the way she yawned, how gorgeous she was when she was all sleepy and tired... And then the transformation of this sleepy woman, who disappeared into her bedroom wearing pyjamas and emerged half an hour later perfectly groomed and smelling amazing!

He enjoyed the chats they would have as they walked to work...the way she'd wrap her hands around a take-out coffee cup...the way her lips would purse as she blew on her drink to cool it...

So many things were getting into his system, making him want to enjoy them more, and—dammit—he didn't know how he wanted to feel about that. This was just meant to be about the baby, but his thoughts were becoming about *her*, too.

He'd never been in a romantic relationship. Not one that had lasted for more than one night, anyway. He knew about attraction. He was a master of desire. But was he any good at doing more than that?

Spent, he pulled himself from the water, the heat rising in steam from his body, and grabbed a towel and headed inside to the changing rooms. His arms and legs hurt in a pleasant way. He'd got his blood moving. He'd had the workout he needed.

Well, the one he would *allow* himself to have.

Time to go back and face temptation all over again.

'You're up?'

Kristjan had come through the front door just as she was getting on her coat, ready for work.

'Yes. Where did you go? I was worried when you weren't here.'

'I left you a note.'

'You did? Where?'

'On the fridge.'

'I didn't see it.'

She went into the kitchen and saw that on the floor, almost out of view, was a green sticky note that must have fallen off the fridge earlier.

'Found it!'

He'd followed her into the kitchen, opened

the fridge and was taking a huge glug of orange juice. 'How are the ankles today?'

'Oh, much better after resting, thank you.'

'You're feeling okay?'

'Absolutely.'

She watched him. He'd come in carrying a bag, and now he picked it up and headed into his own room. He certainly was a mystery man.

'Where did you go?' she called.

'For a swim.'

'In this weather?' she asked in surprise.

He emerged from his room. 'Geothermal pool. Keeps you nice and warm.'

'Oh. I didn't know you swam.'

'I do on occasion.' He smiled and grabbed his jacket. 'Ready?'

'Yes.'

It was a little weird this morning. She could feel the tension between them after last night. It had been hard to lie in her room, staring at the bedroom ceiling, knowing that just a few metres away Kristjan lay in his own bed, wishing he was in hers!

She'd wanted him there too, if she were brutally honest, but her logical mind had kept telling her that it was a good thing that he wasn't. That he had done the honourable thing. Because this situation wasn't about them satisfying their lustful urges for each other—this was about the baby and nothing more. If there'd been no pregnancy she wouldn't even *be* here. She never would have seen him again! He wouldn't have given her a second thought!

No, it was *good* that he was being sensible—because they both needed to be. Right?

Even if, looking at him right now, she could easily imagine what it might be like to throw caution to the wind and satisfy those urges that she was feeling towards him. She could rip off his jacket and push him up against the wall, begin pulling his shirt out from the waistband of his trousers and feel those rock-hard abs once again, and the heat of him in her hands, and...

'Let's go to work.'

She nodded, hoping her hot flush wasn't visible. Work was a good idea. They couldn't do anything at work.

At least that was what she kept repeating to herself as they tramped through the snow towards the hospital.

* * *

The department was busy, which was good, because it kept her occupied and kept her thoughts away from Kristjan. She'd sutured the arm of a twelve-year-old, diagnosed a four-year-old with asthma and another with chicken pox, and now she was seeing to a seven-year-old girl who'd been brought in by her mother because she'd been up all night with tummy pains and being sick.

It could simply be a bug, but children were very good at compensating when there was something else going on in their bodies, and it paid to be thorough. Merry had quickly come to realise that a mother's instinct was usually not wrong.

Would she have that herself? Was it something you learned or was it truly instinctual? She'd followed a hunch before, believed that Mark was her soulmate, that he would treat her as the love of his life until they were old and grey, and she'd got *that* wrong.

'I'm just going to have a feel of your tummy, Ingmar—is that okay?'

Ingmar nodded, looking pale and teary-eyed.

Merry observed the abdomen and then began

to palpate. It quickly became apparent that Ingmar had pain over McBurney's Point, indicating that something was going on with her appendix.

'I think you have appendicitis—which means, Ingmar, that we're going to have to take the appendix out.'

Ingmar looked at her mother, terrified.

'Surgery?' the woman asked.

She nodded at the mum. 'I'm afraid so. It's the safest option. If the appendix ruptures it can cause considerable pain and further difficulties. We need to act sooner, rather than later. When did she last eat?'

'About six o'clock last night,' Agnes translated.

Over twelve hours—that was good. It would lessen any risk with the anaesthetic.

'Good. Okay, so nothing more to eat now, but she can have sips of water if she wants. I'll get a nurse to come and insert a cannula, and get some extra painkillers on board, and then I'll get the surgeons to come down and have a chat with you both.'

'Okay…'

'And I'll come and check on you in the ward

afterwards, when it's all done. You'll be absolutely fine, Ingmar. You're in good hands.'

She laid her hand on the little girl's and gave it a quick squeeze, knowing exactly how Ingmar felt. She'd felt terrified herself when she'd had to have her own appendix out, aged twelve. Back then she'd already been looking after her mum, who had been in a wheelchair, and though Merry had been frightened about the pains she'd been having, she'd thought they were period pains, and had simply stayed quiet until she'd collapsed at the bottom of the stairs.

It had been a terrifying time, but she had lain in the hospital ward worrying more about her mum than herself.

Would Kristjan be at her bedside when she gave birth? Would he hold her hand and help her through her contractions? Would he care and fret and worry over her the way her mother had?

Or would he only be there because of the baby? Because that was what he had said when they were at Ingrid's restaurant last night. That was the true connection between them. The lust and desire they felt was just an urge they both wanted to scratch. Once the itch was gone, what would be left over?

He was on the phone at the doctors' desk, asking for a porter to be bleeped, and she waited for him to get off the phone before asking him her question.

'Do you want to be at the birth?'

He blinked. 'Of course I do!'

'Right. Okay.'

'Do you *want* me at the birth?'

She tried to picture it. Being in pain, struggling through contractions for hours and hours, puffing on gas and air. Doing it alone, with no one at her side, would be...*horrible*. She could hire a doula, but it wouldn't be the same as someone who cared. And she thought that he did—even if it was just for the baby.

'I do,' she said.

He smiled. 'Good.'

She looked down at her booted feet. *It was okay.*

'Have you ever had your appendix out?' she asked.

'No.'

'Ever been in hospital and had to have surgery?'

'No.'

So he *didn't* know what it was like, then.

'But I've sat by lots of bedsides until my patients have woken up and I can know that they're okay.'

Yes. She could imagine him doing that. He was attentive. She would give him that.

'You'll be a good birth partner, then?'

'I'd like to think so. Does that mean you've decided to stay?'

She took a moment to think about it. *Had* she made a decision? It would be hard to say yes, but a part of her really wanted to. Because then the responsibility for this new life would be shared, and she would have someone in her corner again. She'd forgotten what that was like...

I want to be loved.

'I don't know,' she said.

There were carollers in the hospital, in the main foyer, standing beneath the Christmas tree. They wore dark coats, red scarves, and each of them had on a Santa hat with a fluffy white bobble. Their beautiful voices were soaring to the heavens like angels.

Merry stood listening to them, imagining the carollers who had found her outside a vicar's house and what they must have thought... thinking of how carollers had always held a special place in her heart. They went from home to home to try and bring a little pleasure to people by singing their favourite Christmas tunes. It was probably why she'd so easily joined in with the singing at The Elf Foundation.

Right now they were singing an Icelandic version of 'Silent Night', and she wasn't sure whether it was the music, or whether it was the lead female singer, whose voice was absolutely amazing, soaring above the rest, but she felt tears prick the backs of her eyes.

It was such beautiful, heartfelt music.

She felt hands upon her shoulders and turned to see Kristjan there, just standing, listening to the singing, too.

'Isn't it wonderful?' she asked wistfully.

'It is. I thought you didn't like Christmas?'

She smiled and sniffed, wiping away her tears. 'I'm warming to it. And carollers have always been special to me.'

'Because they found you?'

'If they hadn't done what they chose to do I could have died out there in the cold.'

He didn't say anything. He didn't have to. She could feel his thumbs caressing her back.

They didn't need to speak. They just stood there, watching and listening, as the carollers went from 'Silent Night' to 'O Holy Night' and then 'Have Yourself A Merry Little Christmas'.

Merry let out a heavy sigh and turned to face him. 'I need to go and check on my patient. She should be out of surgery now and on the ward.'

'The appendectomy?'

She nodded.

'I'll come with you.'

They rode up in the lift together silently, with Merry very much aware she was in a contained space with Kristjan. He tended to fill small spaces—or at least, to her, he seemed to. It was hard not to be aware of him when he was around. But after the other night, and the way he had held her as they listened to the carol singing just now, it was as if she could still feel his hands upon her body. She craved more of that, and the fact that she knew he was having a hard time keeping his hands off her… Well, that just added to the tension.

It was a nice tension. Electric. Sexual. Her body tingled nicely in anticipation and there was something about knowing she was carrying his child that made her want him even more. She felt that maybe her feelings were moving beyond the sexual too. She liked him. *Really* liked him. She liked being around him. Her heart skipped a beat when she saw him. His smile warmed her…she found herself craving more.

But it was madness to think that they could create a decent relationship between them. Because he didn't do romance, or girlfriends, and she refused ever to get involved romantically with a man again. A relationship based on sexual attraction would never last, because *lust* never lasted, and if they screwed up the nice little friendship they'd got going on right now they'd never forgive themselves. Not when both of them wanted this baby to be brought up by two parents.

The lift doors pinged open and they headed to the recovery ward. Ingmar was in the first bed, with a nurse beside her taking her observations.

'How is she doing?' asked Merry.

'Very well. Temperature and blood pressure are normal. She's just starting to come round.'

'How long before she makes it onto Olaf Ward?'

'A couple of hours.'

'Has the surgeon spoken to the parents?'

'I believe so.'

Merry watched as Ingmar's eyelids flickered slightly before she went back to sleep again. It would take her a few moments to come around properly but children tended to sleep well after anaesthetic. The most important thing was that all had gone well.

She had no other patients in the recovery ward to check on, so she thanked the nurse and headed back to the lifts.

'I had my appendix out when I was twelve,' she said.

Kristjan raised an eyebrow. 'Really?'

'Yes. I remember being really worried about my mum, because she was going through a bad patch with her health.'

'A bad patch?'

'She had Motor Neurone Disease. She was diagnosed in her early forties with amyotrophic lateral sclerosis.'

'I'm sorry. Was it difficult?'

'Incredibly. I didn't know what to do, you know…? I was meant to be looking after her. Yet there I was in a hospital bed and she was having to cope at home all by herself.'

'A child shouldn't have to have such responsibilities.'

'I know—but I did. And it ended up giving me my purpose.'

'Medicine?'

She nodded. 'My mother tried her very best, even when she was at her absolute worst. I hope that I'm able to be the best mother I can be at all times.'

'As long as everyone does their best…that's all we can ask for.'

'Do you think my birth parents did their best? When they abandoned me?'

He thought for a moment. 'I have to hope so. Hope that their own situation wasn't optimal for raising a child and they gave you up so you'd have something better.'

'But why abandon me in the cold? Doesn't

that strike you as uncaring? They could have left me at a hospital, or a fire station, or at a doctor's surgery.'

'Try to look on it with positivity. You may never know the real truth, so you have to choose to believe you were left where they knew you would be found quickly.'

'You're more forgiving than I.'

'It's something I learned to do long ago. Forgive the world.'

He was very sage, but since getting pregnant she'd begun to wonder about her real family. What might she be passing on to her baby genetically? She had no idea.

'I wonder how my child will remember me?'

'I'm sure they will love you very much.'

She smiled, grateful that he was trying to keep her cheered.

'You're worried about the baby, aren't you?' he asked.

She nodded. 'I think I'm more worried about doing it right. Being a mother.'

'We're doing everything we can to make sure he or she is given the best start in life. To make sure that our child is loved and cared for.'

'Are we?'

She wasn't sure if they were. She was still dithering, after all, about staying in Iceland. If she truly wanted to give their baby the best start and both parents wouldn't she have decided to stay by now? Would it be enough for her just to be a co-parent with Kristjan? Or would she spend a lifetime yearning for more, because her fear of loving him was too great?

He reached up to tuck a stray strand of hair behind her ear. He smiled gently at her. 'We are, Merry.'

She still wasn't sure. Something felt very wrong and she couldn't identify it yet. Kristjan's certainty was niggling her and she felt a wave of irritation sweep over her.

Just what the hell was she doing? She'd come all this way to Iceland to tell a man he was going to be a father and then go home. She hadn't intended to do any more than that. Didn't need a man to tell her what to do, and yet she had allowed Kristjan to persuade her to stay until the snow cleared. Then he had asked her to stay on after that and give up her life in the UK, and she was actually *considering* it! After vowing never to let a man call the shots in her life again! Here she was, pandering to what *Kristjan* wanted! She was making the same mistake again. Allowing her attraction to a man to muddy her thinking.

She took a step back. 'This is wrong.'

'What is?'

'This. The whole... *This!* I need some space. I need some perspective. I need...' She saw the surprised look on his face. 'I need to get a clear head. Kristjan. I need to go home.'

'What? I thought you were going to—?'

'Stay? Yes, you thought that because I agreed to it and because I thought I had no choice. But staying here with you isn't allowing me to think straight!'

'Merry...'

'No! This is too much! Working with you, living with you, and now I'm going to raise a baby with you? It's too much, too fast!'

He let out a breath. 'You're panicking.'

'You bet your life I am!'

'What can I do to make this better?'

'Nothing! It's not up to you to make this better! It's not up to you to fix. I need to sort this out on my own!'

Kristjan stared straight at her. 'Why?'

She stared back, suddenly deflated. Confused. 'What do you mean, *why?*'

'Why do you have to sort it on your own? Could it be because that's what you've always done? And because this...this sharing responsibility with someone else...feels odd? *Terrifying?*'

How did he *know*? How did he know that she was scared?

Tears began to fall. From somewhere he produced a handkerchief and then he was guiding her over to a set of chairs.

'I'm scared, too. You think I know what I'm doing? I don't. But neither does any new parent. There's no manual here. There's no set of rules. Everybody makes it up as they go along, from minute to minute.'

Merry felt as if she was about to start hyperventilating, her breathing was coming so fast.

'That's the whole point! I can't get this wrong. I *can't...*'

She could no longer speak. Her breathing was too rapid and she was beginning to feel faint. Her hands were tingling with pins and needles and her chest hurt. It was as if there wasn't enough air.

'Merry?'

She flapped her hands in front of her face, to get more oxygen, but nothing seemed to be working and she couldn't speak to tell him.

But somehow he knew, and he scooped her up in his arms once again and backed through the doors to the recovery ward, laid her on a bed and got an oxygen mask over her mouth.

'Breathe for me, Merry. Breathe… You're having a panic attack.'

She clutched that mask as if it was her only lifeline in the world, sucking in huge lungsful of air as if it was her last ever chance.

'Steady breaths, now. In for five seconds… out for five. Come on, look at me. Look into my eyes and breathe with me. One…two… three…'

She latched on to his steely blue eyes. Once upon a time she would have thought that staring into his eyes was the wrong thing to do, but it was totally *right* now, as she tried to follow his instructions, and slowly, after a few minutes, her breathing became easier.

Her body began to tremble with all the adrenaline that had surged into it. She felt relieved, and also a little embarrassed that she had freaked out so suddenly, but being with him was raking up all these feelings, and she still had no clear answers. She felt as if someone was going to come along at any moment and say, *A baby? You can't have a baby! You have no idea of what you're doing!*

What if she couldn't do it?

She and Kristjan were going through all this and yet when it came along the baby might be too much for her. She might be like her birth mother and…

'Look at me, Merry. Breathe…'

She removed the oxygen mask. 'I'm sorry. I didn't mean to freak out.'

'It's okay.'

'You must think I'm being silly.'

'I don't.'

'What if I can't do this? Be a mum?' she whispered.

Kristjan smiled at her, nothing but kindness and empathy in his eyes.

He sat on the bed, stroked the side of her face and whispered back, 'Oh, Merry! But what if you *can*?'

CHAPTER EIGHT

'I WANT TO show you something. Are you up to going out?'

'Sure. Where are we going?'

Kristjan smiled at Merry, wanting it to be a surprise. 'Somewhere special.'

He helped her on with her coat, wrapped her scarf around her neck and pulled her woolly hat down over her head.

She smiled at him the entire time and he was glad that she was okay now, after her panic attack that afternoon.

He understood her freaking out. Sometimes he wished he could do the same thing, but she needed someone strong beside her whilst she worked through this. They both did. Luckily, they had each other. Although he didn't think Merry understood just how much he needed *her*, too. It was a realisation that totally freaked *him* out.

But he was managing. Minute by minute. Hour by hour.

After today he'd figured she needed to see something amazing. And tonight was meant to be a good night, by all accounts.

'Can you trust me?' he asked.

'It depends.'

'I want you to wear this blindfold.' He held up another scarf.

She laughed. 'This isn't *Fifty Shades*, Kristjan.'

He smiled. 'I know. This is nothing like that, but I want where we're going to be a surprise. I promise you'll be safe and if at any time you feel you need to take it off, then I won't stop you.'

She considered it for a moment. 'All right.'

So he tied the scarf around her eyes and guided her out of the house and onto the snow sled. 'Hold on tight—we're off for a short ride to the other side of Wonderland.'

'What's there?'

'Everything.' He knew she'd like it once she saw it. He knew she needed to see it, too.

Starting the engine, he drove them to the special place just beyond Wonderland. Here was the real countryside of Iceland, and there was one spot that lots of people went to, to see something really special as there was no other light pollution to get in the way.

Parked, he slowly helped her off the snow sled and gently guided her to where she needed to stand. He looked up at the sky above them, knowing that this would be perfect, and then he slowly removed the scarf from her eyes, watching her face attentively as he did so. He wanted to see her reaction. Wanted her to see the beauty. Wanted her to see what *he* saw.

'The Aurora Borealis!' she gasped.

Above them, green and blue waves arced across the sky as if blown by a solar wind, slowly dancing to an unknown tune, glimmering and flickering from dark green to light, as if mixed by invisible fingers. There was a hint of yellow at the outermost edges, swirling like mist.

'It's like magic!'

He watched her face, her smile, her awe. The gleam in her eyes at seeing such a natural wonder.

'Beautiful, indeed.'

He looked up, watching the lights as they

rolled and flowed above them. They were caused by disturbances in the magneto-sphere—charged particles emitting light and ionisation. He knew the science, he knew the facts, but it was still a wondrous display... almost mystical.

'This is amazing, Kristjan! Thank you!'

'You needed to see it. To see the wonder of the world. How beautiful it is. In our job we get to see a lot of pain. A lot of upset. It can be scary, and I don't want you to be scared ever again.'

She turned to him. Looked up into his eyes. He could see the lights reflected in her pupils. She looked as if she had magic swirling inside her, and in a way she did. She was growing their baby.

He couldn't help himself. He took a step to-wards her, cupped her face in his hands and brought her lips to his. They were soft. Warm. And she sank into him, against him, her tongue entwining with his as he deepened the kiss.

He didn't need the light show above. There were fireworks going off inside him. He'd dreamt of this. Wanted this ever since she'd walked through the doors of the hospital, freezing cold and dripping wet, dragging that suitcase. It had been a sweet torture to see her each day. An ache in his soul, an agony that he had to keep his distance—and, boy, had he tried! He had tried so hard. And now, in the night-time air, with wind so cold and biting it felt as if it was slicing at his skin, he was blissfully ignorant as his body temperature soared at her touch.

He hadn't kissed her like this since Hawaii. From that tropical beach to this heart of winter she made the rest of the world fall away, and all he could think of—all he knew as his lips joined with hers—was ecstasy.

'Merry…'

He traced his lips along the length of her jaw, down her neck, but that damned scarf was in the way! He wanted to rip it off her, just as much as he wanted to rip away all their clothes, but they were out in the freezing cold and that wouldn't do. He knew he needed to have her— he couldn't wait any longer.

Her pupils had grown large and dark, her lips were swollen from his kisses, and she looked at him in a daze.

'Take my hand.'

He guided her back to the snow sled, waited for her to get on it and wrap her arms around his waist, and then they were off—heading for home...where there was warmth and beds and a hot shower.

He reminded himself to be careful. Not to rush. He carried precious cargo with him and, although he was adept with a motorised sled, he'd seen plenty of ferocious injuries to kids who had come off them, or overturned them, or simply gone too fast and not read the lie of the land beneath the snow. There was a certain skill to it. A sixth sense, almost. You had to work *with* the snow, not against it.

The lights of the Borealis were left behind them as the lights and noise of Wonderland grew ever closer. He saw the happy families, heard the music. Normally he would have enjoyed it—slowed down and taken in the sight—but not tonight.

He felt her arms tighten around him and he pressed one gloved hand against hers, clutching it to his chest. He drove like that for quite a way, until he had to let go to steer them home. As they got closer and closer it was as if he could hear his heart thundering in his head. He felt hot. Ready to strip himself of his clothes and bury himself in her. To devour her. To be consumed by her.

He parked, helped her off and, still holding her hand, led her inside. Once the door was closed he helped unwind her scarf and unzip her coat. Then he pulled off her woolly hat and he gazed at her with a smile. 'Are you sure?'

She nodded.

It was all the permission he needed.

She hadn't known what to expect when he'd blindfolded her. It had been a difficult day, what with her panic attack, but when he'd removed the scarf and she'd seen the Northern Lights... It had been as if a miracle had occurred in the sky. As if she was watching real magic. And, even though logically she knew there was a scientific reason for what had been happening, and that it could easily be explained, she'd preferred just to stand there and soak it in, wondering at the wonderful display it was, believing it would be the pinnacle of her evening.

She had been wrong.

Kristjan had kissed her. And it had been as

if he had switched on fairy lights in her body. Because now she was burning hot and bright all over and she wanted him more than ever. The short ride back to the house had been wonderful—leaning into him, her arms wrapped around him—and he had taken her hand, and she had thought she could feel the thudding of his heart inside his chest.

And now they were inside, and he was kissing her again, and—*oh, my God*—it was everything. She felt dizzy and senseless and all of a quiver, with a sharp need that she knew could only be sated by him.

She needed his mouth upon her body. She needed him to touch her as she had never been touched before. And she reached down to lift up her jumper and toss it to one side.

Why am I wearing so many layers?

After the jumper there was a shirt, and beneath that a thermal top. There were jeans and her thick socks, and then there were all *his* clothes. They tried to shed them as fast as they could, but jeans got caught on ankles and needed a tug, which made them both laugh, and then he couldn't get his shirt off without undoing the cuffs. And although Merry had never imagined herself as a woman who might actually want to physically *rip* the clothes off another person, she found herself wanting to do that so badly!

And then finally—*finally!*—they were down to their underwear, and suddenly everything slowed right down...which was perfect.

He traced the strap of her bra from her shoulder down to her breast, his thumb brushing over her peaked nipple through the lace before he stooped to kiss and suck it through the thin material.

Oh, my God!

She arched back, thrusting her breasts further towards him, the agony and the ecstasy of it all making her act on animal instinct. She felt his thumbs hook into the sides of her knickers and he slowly slid them down her legs, his lips tracing a trail of soft, featherlight kisses over her belly and her abdomen and her sex, where his tongue lingered, licking and teasing as she quivered above him.

Why had she denied herself this? Why had she fought this for so long?

It had been impossible to forget how good it had been between them in Hawaii, and it had given her some delicious dreams in the weeks afterwards. Before she knew about the baby she had often thought about how it might be if they were ever to run into each other again.

Yet they had *both* tried to not do this. Tried not to sleep with one another again. Because they hadn't wanted to complicate matters. But here they were. He was lowering her down onto the rug in front of the fire that had been slowly kindling whilst they were out and she could feel its gentle warmth down one side of her body as Kristjan created a trail of pleasuring kisses.

His muscles gleamed and rippled in the firelight, his arms flexing with power as he held himself easily above her. The whiskers from his beard tickled her inner thighs and she felt him caress her lower abdomen, stroking tenderly with his fingertips where the baby was before he came up to kiss her again.

She could taste herself in his kiss and she responded fully, wanting more of him, wrapping her legs around his back and pulling him closer. 'I need you, Kristjan. Now.'

He gazed into her eyes for a moment. 'I don't have any protection on me.'

She smiled. 'You can't get me pregnant. I already am.'

'But what about—?'

'I'm clean. I haven't slept with anyone but you.'

She could see that he was deciding what to tell her. Whether to admit to the truth, or not. The truth won out. 'Nor me—not since Hawaii.'

She smiled. 'Really? There's been no one since me?'

He smiled back. 'No. But it would be irresponsible to assume...'

'Please, Kristjan... I need you *now*.'

When he entered her she felt the full length of him filling her up and she groaned, arching upwards, clutching him to her, pulling his lips down onto her own, needing to consume him as he consumed her.

His movements were slow and languid at first, so that she felt pleasure in every single millisecond, every delicious inch, before his movements got quicker and quicker and he clutched at her bottom, pulling her against him as he powered into her again and again.

Merry allowed herself to sink into it, her

arms outstretched above her head, breathing hard and heavy with every thrust.

This was what sex was meant to be like.

Feeling the way she did right now, she knew that what she'd had before had been nothing. Mark had been a bad amateur, not really knowing how to pleasure a woman and only considerate of how *he* felt.

Kristjan took her to the brink, and each time she thought she might come he slowed it down and withdrew, kissing her, nibbling, licking, leaving her gasping with delight and desire, before plunging in again so that when she finally came, in a explosion of ecstasy, he came himself.

They lay spent together afterwards, wrapped in each other's arms on the rug in front of the gently crackling fire. Merry put her head on the rise and fall of his chest, her fingers tickling the chest hair there.

Everything ached in such a wonderful way. Her every nerve-ending was alive and shining bright like stars in a night sky. She fitted against him as if she had been made specifically just for him. She felt so happy. So content.

There was no need for talk. Their bodies

had said everything they needed to say. And they fell asleep in front of the fire, wrapped together, legs entwined.

When she woke in the early hours of the morning, she found that Kristjan had got up already, but he had laid a lovely blanket of red and white over her and gently stoked the fire, laying it with fresh logs to keep her warm.

There was a note beside her.

Gone for a swim. Back soon. K

She smiled, pulling herself up into a seated position, clutching the blanket to her naked chest. She was hungry, and thirsty, and as if he had known what she would need there was a tray laid on the small coffee table. A pot of coffee. A pot of hot chocolate. Some pastries and a bowl of fresh fruit.

Thought you might need this. K

The note was stuck to one of the Christmas pudding mugs that she was now so familiar with seeing about the place.

She would eat and then grab a shower, she thought. Looking at the clock, she saw they had three hours before they both needed to be at work.

They had taken a huge step forward last night, and Kristjan had shown her that he wanted to be with her. That was massive. For both of them. It must have been so obvious that there was something simmering away between them. It had been palpable—even the people at work had noticed, she felt sure.

It was the beginning of something. A way forward. One step taken. All the pair of them could do was take it one day at a time.

Kristjan powered through the water in a front crawl, barely stopping, his arms slicing through the heated water of the geothermal pool as if they were blades. His chest was protesting and he was gasping for air, but it was as if he was punishing himself, seeing how far he could go, and for how long, without taking a breath, knowing he wouldn't stop until his body forced him to.

He had slept with Merry. And when he'd woken this morning he hadn't known how he felt about that.

The sex had been great. It had been before

and he had no doubt that it always would be. But…

Relationships were never just about sex.

Relationships were…*expectations*.

When you were with someone, when you were committed, that other person expected certain things. By sleeping with Merry had he given her the impression that they were something bigger? Because last night, for him, it had been all about sating the lust that he'd felt since he'd laid eyes on her again and had started getting to know her a bit more. Since he'd had her in *his* house, in *his* guest bedroom, under *his* roof, knowing that she was carrying *his* baby…

His lungs burned and he stopped, gasping for air, steam rising from the warmth of his skin in the cold morning air. All around him snow lay on the surface at the poolside, on the benches where people could sit, on the rails where they draped their towels. It was freezing, and yet he felt none of it. His thoughts were enmeshed with what had happened and what it might mean.

Merry wouldn't expect anything of him, would she? She'd told him before that she would never make the same mistake again and get into a relationship simply because of lust—and wasn't *lust* the emotion that had driven them both last night?

He was in the clear, right? They'd both simply scratched an insatiable itch and now everything would be fine. They'd be clear-headed. Able to think straight.

But all his mind could focus on was a replay of last night. The way her skin had looked in the firelight. The smooth curves of her flesh. The softness. The roundness of her lower abdomen where their baby grew. The taste of her...

He felt his body stir in response and, feeling aggravated that it was doing that, he pulled himself from the water and lay down on the poolside, rolling himself in the snow. He'd hoped the shock of the cold would sort him out and cleave those thoughts from his brain as his body went into survival mode. Only it never happened.

He simply remembered her gasps. Her breathing. How she'd arched against him and how it had felt to hear her scream his name... Even now, his body reacted! He'd hoped that by being with her at last he would finally get some control back over his feelings, but it was as if she had fed them and they had grown and they wanted to be fed again.

Would it ever stop?

If she left—if she went back to the UK—would he finally feel his body chill out and stop reacting to the thought of her?

But I don't want her to go back to the UK.

Perhaps they both needed some space? She was living in his house. She was at his place of work. What if he found her another place to stay? He had lots of friends who might have a spare room or a couch…

But did he really want the mother of his baby sleeping on someone's couch? The answer was a resounding no. She deserved the comfort of her own bed.

Maybe I should be the one to move out?

He thought of perhaps spending a few nights in the on-call rooms. He'd done it before. And the hospital always got busier around the Christmas period—especially as the big day got closer. It would be a good reason to stay there without her thinking that he was avoiding her. And when he *had* to spend time with her he could take her to places that didn't involve being near a bedroom. Show her the local schools and nurseries. Give her an idea of what it would be like for their baby to live in Snowy Peak as it grew up. Prove to her that there was a *future* here.

It seemed reasonable to him. It certainly seemed like a plan. And he felt badly in need of one of those.

Kristjan draped his towel around his shoulders and brushed off some of the snow. Three days till Christmas. Their first Christmas together, the two of them alone. After this there would be a baby to consider.

He hoped that they would at least spend it sitting around the same table. The thought that they might not be able to…pained him. But he had to be realistic. He was getting too close to her. Letting his feelings for her overwhelm him. If he lost her and the baby now, how would that feel?

He stared at the snow-covered mountain.

No. It was already too much loss to contemplate. He couldn't lose them. No matter how damn scary it was to keep her close.

* * *

'He's had a fever for a couple of days, with a cold, but today his temperature has been sky-high, and he's all sleepy, so…'

'You did the right thing, bringing him in.' Kristjan reassured the mother as he grabbed hold of an electronic thermometer to check the baby boy's temperature for himself.

He put on a single use cover and placed the probe in the boy's ear. It beeped and he checked the temperature. Thirty-nine point six.

'Hmm…that's very high. Just over a hundred and three. Has he had any rashes that you've noticed?'

'Not really. One or two spots, but…'

'Where?'

'On his belly.'

The baby was ten months old and currently wearing only a sleeveless vest over his nappy. Kristjan lifted the clothing and noticed a bit of a mottled discolouration on the baby's skin that didn't look good.

'Has he been having plenty of wet nappies?'

'Not as many as he usually does—but then he hasn't been drinking as much. What do you think it is? A virus?'

He hoped that was all it was, but right now Kristjan was worried about sepsis—a life-threatening reaction to an infection...the immune system overreacting. The baby was breathing quite rapidly. But he didn't want to alarm the mother unless he was sure.

'Was he born at term? After a healthy pregnancy?'

'He was born a month early.'

'Right. And he's up to date with his vaccinations?'

'Yes.'

'Okay. I'm worried that his body is overreacting to an infection, so what I'm going to do is admit him and give him strong antibiotics and some fluids.'

'You think it's serious?'

'It could be. It might be sepsis. And if it is then I want us to be fighting it as soon as we can, okay?'

'Okay.'

The mum looked worried, but she was remaining calm, which was great.

'I'm admitting him right now. A nurse will come in to start the antibiotics and she'll monitor him until we can get him up to a ward.'

'Thank you, Doctor.'

'No problem. You did a good thing bringing him in.'

He headed from the cubicle to chart the case immediately, to prescribe the antibiotics and to call up to not only the children's ward but also the intensive care unit, to make sure they had space if necessary—which they did. Then he asked a nurse to take a blood sample, so they could send it off for some rapid testing.

'I want observations every fifteen minutes.'

The nurse nodded.

'Good morning!' The voice came from behind him.

He looked up. *Merry.* 'Good morning.'

'You were gone when I woke up.'

She leaned in over the counter and he breathed in her perfume. It did some heady things to his senses, and it was all he could do not to reach over the counter and pull her closer.

'I went for a swim and then I came in early.'

'Thanks for leaving me some breakfast.'

Oh. He'd forgotten about that.

'No problem.'

He wished he'd been there to feed it to her.

Mouthful by mouthful, teasing those lips of hers with strawberries and other delightful things.

He watched her look around them before leaning in closer and whispering, 'I had a good time last night.'

So did I. 'Me too.'

'And we're okay?'

He smiled. 'Of course. Why wouldn't we be?'

'Good. I thought I might cook you dinner tonight? And for dessert we could…'

Her voice trailed off and he knew what she was implying.

She meant sex. More sex. And normally he wasn't the type of guy who would turn down sex with a woman he really wanted.

'Sounds good. I'd love to stop and think about that a bit more thoroughly, but I've got a query sepsis case I need to process.'

She nodded, understanding instantly. 'Don't let me stop you.'

He grabbed the notes and headed off in the direction of the young baby's cubicle, to update the mother and get the antibiotics on board. He didn't need to do it himself—the nurse was more than capable—but he needed to get away. To keep his head clear and in the zone for treating patients.

He couldn't afford to be distracted.

In her lunch hour, Merry decided to go Christmas shopping. Christmas was only a couple of days away, and she felt she needed to get Kristjan a present or two. He'd done so much for her—giving her a place to stay, a job to go to—and he was still doing his best to get her to stay in Iceland.

He deserved a gift. Something thoughtful. Something that would make him smile. And perhaps after dinner tonight she would give him the best present of all…

It didn't take her long to find a shop that sold fancy underwear. Silk. Lace. She tried on one or two pieces before making her selection, and then headed off to get him something that he wouldn't be allowed to see until the twenty-fifth of December.

It was difficult. She wasn't sure what to get him. He had bookshelves, but they were mainly filled with medical books, and he played his music through a speaker, so there wasn't any music collection she could plough through. She knew he dressed well, and enjoyed swimming, his job...

Maybe something for The Elf Foundation?

A thought struck her, but she knew it wasn't something she could get sorted in a lunch hour. She needed to head back to the hospital, but when she got back she'd search the internet for someone to help her with her idea and make a few calls, put it into motion...

She felt very happy with her decision, and couldn't wait to see Kristjan's face when he found out. Now all she had to do was get through the afternoon, cook dinner, and then let him unwrap her like a very special present!

But first she had a list of patients. She picked up the chart at the top of the pile, checked that Agnes was free to accompany her, and then headed through to a cubicle, to see a woman sitting on the examination bed next to a little boy who was reading a book.

'Hello. I'm Dr Bell. What's brought you in here today?'

'I couldn't get in to see my local doctor, so I've brought my son here. He's got all these bruises. Look at them! On his arms...his legs.

You should see the ones he has on his back! He wasn't like that when I dropped him off at his father's house a couple of days ago.'

Merry understood the subtext. This mother was suggesting that her ex-partner was either neglectful, or that he was abusing the boy. Well…it could be either of those—or neither. It could be something medical, she knew, but clearly the boy's mother hadn't considered that.

'I want you to take photographs. I've got some on my phone, but I want this reported!'

'Okay…well, let's take a look first, shall we?'

The boy's name was Tómas and he was six years of age. Old enough to co-operate, if he wasn't too scared.

'Hey, Tómas. Can I have a look at you?' she asked.

The boy nodded and put down his book.

'What are you reading?'

'It's about pirates. And a dragon.'

'Wow! Sounds amazing! You like to read?'

'Yes.'

'Me, too! But I can't remember the last book I read that had a dragon in it. Or a pirate, for that matter. Is he a good pirate?'

'He's okay.'

The boy really did have some bruises on him, but they didn't look like hand marks, or the kind of bruises he'd get if someone had held him tightly. They were mostly small. The kind of bruises she'd expect a rough and tumble young boy to have. But he did have a lot, and the one on his side, near his back, was quite big.

'Did you fall over at your dad's?'

'No.'

'Did you play any sports?'

'We went ice-skating.'

'Sounds fun. And you didn't fall over there?'

'I nearly fell over. I hit the side of the rink when someone crashed into me.'

'Uh-huh…'

It could just be a collision injury, but Merry's sixth sense was tingling, telling her something wasn't right here. The boy looked quite pale, and he was a little underweight. If this was abuse, she'd be surprised.

'How have you been feeling lately, Tómas? Your usual self?'

'He's been tired,' the mother answered. 'Like he's got no energy. He wasn't very keen on going to his dad's…he wanted to stay home.'

More subtext. The mum was willing her to understand her suspicions.

'Is that right? You've been feeling tired? Sleepy?' asked Merry.

'Stuff hurts.'

'What stuff?'

Tómas shrugged. 'Everything.'

Merry looked at his mum. 'Do you brush his teeth for him?'

'No, he does it himself. He's always been very good at that.'

'When you brush your teeth, Tómas, do you notice any bleeding?'

'Only if he does it too hard,' the mum interrupted.

Merry felt around the boy's neck, checking for swollen lymph nodes, and found a couple in the boy's neck. This was definitely something.

'And he's normally fit and well?'

'Absolutely.'

'Okay. The nurse is going to perform a blood test. It's just a small needle—what we call a butterfly needle—and it won't hurt at all.'

'What are you checking for?' asked the mother.

'I want to check his red and white blood

cells, and then I think we may need to get a haematologist to check the results, just to be on the safe side.'

'And then you'll report it?'

'Not yet. Let's see the results of the blood test first, okay?'

The boy's mum nodded reluctantly and Merry watched as Agnes took a sample of blood.

Tómas was very good. He was fascinated by the cold spray the nurse applied to the crook of his elbow and he even watched the needle go in.

'Is that my blood?' he askd.

'It is.'

'Wow!'

She labelled the bottles, marked the request form to check for a range of conditions, and then placed a plaster on his arm, once the bleeding had stopped. It took a little longer than normal, but she tried not to let it show how that worried her. If she was right—and she sincerely hoped that she wasn't—then this wonderful little boy had a type of leukaemia.

'Okay, you can stay here. I'll just get these sent off to the path lab. Tómas? When I come back, I want you to tell me what's happened in your story.'

He smiled at her rather wanly. 'I will.'

Merry closed the curtain, her heart filling with dread as she popped the blood into the shuttle that would send the sample directly to the lab within seconds. When it had whooshed away in the tube, she sat down at the doctors' desk to write up her notes.

'How's it going?' Kristjan appeared from around the corner.

'Not great. How was your case? Was it sepsis?'

'No. I think it's just a nasty virus, but we're keeping the baby in to monitor him. What are you dealing with?'

She sighed and sagged in her chair. 'I'm hoping it's not a case of acute leukaemia.'

Kristjan frowned. 'I'm sorry... Need any help with it?'

'No. I've got the bloods sent off. But... You know when you have that feeling in your gut?'

'I do.'

'Well, I'm hoping mine is wrong.'

'Did you mark the tests as urgent?'

'Yeah.'

'Need a hug?'

She looked up at him and smiled. 'Yeah.'

Kristjan came from around to her side of the desk and wrapped her in a huge bear hug, pressing her gently against his chest so that she felt warm and protected and soothed by his presence. It was nice. It was *very* nice. And she really didn't want him to let go. How quickly she had begun to love being in his arms.

'Do we all get one of those?' asked Agnes, with a smile.

'If you need one,' answered Kristjan.

Merry inhaled his scent one last time, then pushed herself reluctantly away. 'Thanks.'

'No problem.'

'I guess all I can do is wait, huh?'

'And keep your fingers crossed.'

She nodded as he walked away to carry on with his own work, and for a brief moment she crossed her fingers and looked up at the big fat Santa ornament on the doctors' desk.

'If you've got anything to do with this whatsoever,' she whispered urgently, 'then please, *please*, I beg of you, give that family a happy Christmas.'

She wouldn't know if her plea was answered. At least not for a little while.

And when the haematologist himself came down with the results, a grim look on his face, Merry knew that not all prayers were answered.

'You need to do a bone marrow biopsy,' she said.

She just knew.

He nodded, face still grim.

'Okay. Let's go and tell them the news.'

CHAPTER NINE

TÓMAS'S CASE AFFECTED her all afternoon. It was horrible to hear such a life-changing diagnosis at any time of life, but that young... And so close to Christmas...

Merry wondered what kind of a time the family would have, knowing what their youngest child would face after the festive season.

Remission induction to start with, to kill the harmful cells in Tómas's bone marrow, restore the balance and hopefully relieve some of the symptoms. This would be done through blood transfusions, mostly, but it would leave the boy with no immune system.

Then there would be something they called 'consolidation,' to kill any remaining leukaemia cells, and finally maintenance, when he would receive regular chemotherapy treatments to stop the leukaemia from coming back.

His little body would come under attack

from all the medication they'd have to give him, as well as steroids for a couple of years, but hopefully the treatment would work, and he wouldn't suffer any complications.

He and his family had a long road ahead of them, and as she'd worked Merry wondered how she would feel if *her* child ever got terribly sick like that? How would she cope? Would she feel powerless? At the mercy of other doctors and their opinions?

It was something she always tried to keep at the forefront of her mind when she dealt with patients and their families—how would *she* feel to be receiving this news and how would *she* want the doctors to speak to *her*? And now she was thinking would it be better to hear that news alone, or with Kristjan?

He would be strong, no doubt. He would support her, do everything that was needed. And, if either she or their child needed it, he'd be there to give one of those special hugs.

She could see so many benefits to being with him, but it didn't boil down just to pros and cons at the end of the day, did it? It came down to feelings, and hers were all over the place—betraying her, making her want him, making her desire more than they currently had. It was confusing. Dizzying.

She was dreaming of having the fairy tale. Of walking into the sunset with him. Getting her happy-ever-after. Didn't she deserve one after all this time?

So she was hopeful about the situation between herself and Kristjan. They'd turned a corner, hadn't they? Grown closer. Taken a big step in their relationship. And she knew that if she was going to enjoy this evening—which she very much hoped she would—she would have to shake off her feelings about Tómas. He had been sent home now, but would be back the next day for his bone marrow biopsy. All she could do was hope they'd caught it early and that treatment would be effective.

She got home ahead of Kristjan and began preparing their evening meal. She'd decided to try and make something traditional to Iceland. Something heart-warming that would show him that she cared and had made an effort.

Whilst it cooked she took the time to have a quick shower and shave her legs and paint her nails. She was just blowing air over her fingertips when she heard the front door open.

'I'm back!'

'I'll be out in just a minute!'

Excitement and anticipation filled her at the thought of the two of them alone once again. He'd left so early that morning—cheating her out of waking up in his arms—and then they'd spent the day at work, with stressful cases for both of them. Illness and disease didn't care what time of year it was. It happened no matter what. But she could make time and plan for enjoying herself, and she knew she wanted to take time to enjoy Kristjan.

Her nails now dry, she slipped a dress over the fancy underwear she'd bought earlier and padded out barefoot to greet him.

He was standing in the living area, on the rug they'd made love on the night before, loosening his tie. Smiling, she went over to him and went up on tiptoe to give him a welcoming kiss. His beard whiskers tickled for a moment, and then she helped him undo the tie, tossing it over the back of a chair.

'Welcome home.'

'Something smells good.'

'It's a fish stew. *Ploppfishur?*'

He laughed. 'Close enough. Do I have time to take a shower?'

She thought about it. She could turn the heat down a little on the stew. 'I could join you…'

He smiled. 'Really?'

'Mmm… Really.' She stepped closer and began undoing his shirt buttons. 'Let me help you with this shirt.'

Her fingers made quick work of the buttons, and she looked up at him and smiled as her hands dipped lower and lower with each button. Then she pulled his shirt from the waistband of his trousers.

'And with this belt…'

The belt undid easily, and she pulled it from the loops like a whip. Kristjan stared down at her, his breath quickening, as she peeled the shirt from his broad shoulders.

She took in the round curve of his deltoid muscles and leaned in to inhale his delicious scent and lay her lips upon the hot flesh of his chest. She pulled the shirt down his arms and let it drop to the floor, and then she hooked a finger into the top of his trousers and smiled at him.

'Come with me.'

Feeling her body tingling in anticipation, she led him towards his en-suite bathroom and reached in to turn on the shower. Then, with the hiss of the water behind them, she began to undo her dress, pulling loose the tie belt at the waist so that it fell open to reveal the black silk underwear she'd bought earlier.

'You like?'

'Very much so.' His voice husky.

'How about you take a closer look?'

She took his hands, lifted them to her breasts and let go, closing her eyes in delicious agony as she felt his thumbs sweep over her nipples before rising to pull the bra straps from her shoulders. He stepped closer, reaching round her to undo the hook at the back and then slip the bra off.

She smiled at him, hooked her thumbs in the waistband of her knickers and pulled them down, stepping neatly out of them and watching in delight as his gaze hungrily roamed her body.

When he made eye contact once again she stepped forward and undid the button and the zip of his trousers. She reached in beneath his underwear, to take him in her grasp.

He sucked in a breath and she stood there stroking him, feeling him swell in her firm grip, and she smiled like a devil, pleased with her own power.

This was like being back in Hawaii—that very first night when they had first met. They had been equals. Each taking their pleasure. Exploring one another for the first time. Learning what they liked.

Well, Merry knew what *he* liked. 'Do you want more?'

'I do.' His voice was rough, throaty.

She pulled her hand free and began to slide his trousers down, her mouth dropping kisses all the way down his chest, over his abdomen, whispering in featherlight touches over his obliques knowing he was ticklish there as she pulled down his underwear and took him in her mouth.

She had never felt more powerful than she did in that moment. Knowing he was at her mercy and he was all hers. She'd never had this before.

With her husband Mark she had been a passive participant. He'd never needed anything from her except her ability to lie there until he was done. He hadn't wanted her to touch him, to actively give him pleasure, and the first time she had tried he had scowled and told her that he didn't like it. That her being 'sexually aggressive' as he'd called it, turned him off. To him, the male was the leader during sex and she should know her place.

It had been a very unsatisfying sex life, and she had been glad when she'd been able to flee his grasp.

Meeting Kristjan in Hawaii had been a revelation for her. She had explored her own power and what she was capable of doing and it had been refreshing to discover that during intimacy she could ask for things. She could do things she had never tried before. And with every gasp of breath Kristjan had simply signalled to her that she was more powerful than she had ever believed.

Being intimate with Kristjan had given her power. She'd thrived on it. And in turn she'd been vulnerable and had opened up to Kristjan, who was so experienced in pleasuring a woman, and known that she could give up control and it would be okay. He'd made her feel safe. He'd made her feel adventurous. He'd made her feel *equal*.

Now she led Kristjan under the spray of water and their lips met. There was something delicious about the heat of the water on their alert, anticipatory bodies. Every nerve-ending was awaiting his touch as she felt the force and heat of the water pound down upon them, and she was barely aware of the coldness of the black marble tiles as Kristjan pressed her against them, her hands above her head as his lips traced the curve of her neck and shoulder. Her breasts were straining outward, desperate for the caress of his hands and mouth.

'Kristjan...' she breathed.

He lifted her up, pulled her legs around his waist as he thrust into her, grinding into her over and over.

Merry allowed herself to submit to all the delicious feelings in her body. Her tingling nerve-endings. The feel of his mouth upon hers. His large strong hands cupping her buttocks. The water raining down and the feel of him filling her, sliding in and out.

She could feel her orgasm coming, could feel her excitement building, and she clutched him ever tighter, urging him on. Suddenly her world exploded in a firework display of ecstasy and excitement, with Kristjan coming only seconds afterwards.

The water continued to pound down as he slowly lowered her feet to the floor of the shower and kissed her gently—her neck, her breasts, her mouth. And then he was holding her face, cupping it in his hands as he kissed her reverently.

'I've never had dessert before my main course before.'

Merry chuckled. 'And what did you think of it?'

He smiled, smoothing back her hair from her face. 'I could definitely make it a habit.'

They had both eaten ravenously afterwards, having second and even third helpings of Merry's fish stew. She was a good cook, and Kristjan liked it that she was trying new things.

Life was going well for them, he thought. They got on at home and at work. The sex was great! And he enjoyed her company even when they *weren't* lying in each other's arms.

But for now they were. Kristjan was spooning Merry's naked body once again, and the heat of their bodies was making them feel like one.

He could get used to this. Who knew there were delights to be had when you slept with a woman more than once? He'd always thought of sex as something that was a one-off experience. You had your fun and then you forgot about that woman because there was no point in carrying on. In fact, he'd told himself it was *dangerous* to do so.

He'd *never* done this! And he was surprised at how comfortable it made him feel, knowing he could take the time to explore Merry's body. To enjoy it. Even without sex there was something wonderful about just lying here in her arms. It made him feel...*valued*. It wasn't just a desirous wanting, or a need that he felt—though he did feel that too—it was as if she had *chosen* him. Out of all the men on the planet, she had chosen and found worth in *him*. Not just once. Not just in a fleeting sexual encounter never to be experienced again. But multiple times. She was staying. She wanted him.

At least for now, anyway.

'It's Christmas Eve tomorrow,' he said.

'I know. The year has gone so fast.'

'On Christmas Eve here, families usually give each other the gift of a book and sit and read in the evening.'

'They do? What kind of books do you like?'

'I don't know. I've only ever given books to patients before, and I only read for knowledge. It's been a long time since I had a family.'

She turned to look at him, stroked his face. 'You think of us as a family?'

'Aren't we? In some strange way?'

Merry smiled. 'I guess... I'll get you a book. Tell me what you like.'

'I don't know... Crime? Thriller?'

'I'll get you *something.*'

He kissed the tip of her nose. He was grateful to have her here, knowing it could still be fleeting. He thought about the news he'd heard just before he'd left work today. He had to tell her. It was the right thing to do.

'They think they'll be able to clear the mountain pass soon,' he told her.

She'd promised to stay until the roads cleared, but that had been before they'd got closer. Had she changed her mind? Did it even matter to her about the roads? She hadn't said anything.

Did he feel her stiffen slightly? Tense?

He sank his nose into her hair, breathed in her scent. Honey blossom. Meadows. She smelt of freedom and the warmth of summer.

'When?' she asked.

His heart sank. Did she still plan on leaving? Even though she lay here in his arms? He didn't want to lose her, but she was a free woman and he wouldn't tie her down. Mark had restricted her movements; he wouldn't do the same. He had to trust that she would make the right decision.

'I don't know. A nurse mentioned it. She's been hoping to get down to visit her family in Reykjavik.'

'Oh...'

She pulled his arm tighter around her waist and he took that moment to inhale her scent once again, telling himself that if he trapped the memory in his head he would always be able to feel her near. Always remember this moment in which he had held her in his arms. He hoped this wasn't the last time. But he wanted to be honest with her. He didn't want her to hear that he'd known about the roads and chosen not to tell her.

Kristjan closed his eyes, hoping for the peaceful oblivion of sleep, where none of this mattered. Where he didn't live in a world where she might leave him behind. Where he didn't feel the tight fear of her possible desertion in the pit of his gut. Didn't have that sick feeling that he had had recently, the more he had allowed himself to have feelings. The more he lost control.

But sleep wouldn't come.

And he lay there for hours, hoping that Merry wasn't already planning in her head for the time when they would separate. Hoping that telling her the news about the mountain pass wasn't the worst thing he'd ever done in his entire life.

CHAPTER TEN

CHRISTMAS EVE MORNING, and Merry didn't have work until the afternoon—which was good, as there were a few things she needed to sort out in order to give Kristjan the present she was organising. But as she bustled about from place to place in Snowy Peak she couldn't help but ruminate on the fact that he'd told her last night that the mountain pass might soon give safe passage through the mountain range and back to Reykjavik.

Where the airport was.

She could go home.

If I want to.

When she'd first got here it had been all she could think about, but now...? Now everything was muddled. Confused. She didn't know *what* she felt. Her feelings for Kristjan were complicated now, and their situation... She had no idea what to do for the best.

If she stayed, what would it mean for them?

She *loved* it here in Snowy Peak. She could easily admit that she had fallen in love with the place—the area, the people, the hospital…

Kristjan?

She loved being with him. Loved being in his arms. Loved working with him.

But was it any more than that? Was she *in love* with him?

Merry didn't want to be. All these years of telling herself never to get involved with a man again and here she was—in deep with the father of her baby!

As she sat with a latte in one of the coffee shops, she watched the families passing by outside, doing last-minute shopping for friends and family. She watched mothers holding the hands of excited children. She watched fathers as they gave their children shoulder rides to keep them out of the snow. Watched how they would gather snowballs and throw them at each other.

Would this be her future, her baby's future, if she stayed here?

If she did stay, just what would she be committing to?

She and Kristjan hadn't made any rules,

hadn't told each other what they were to one another. Was she reading too much into what was happening? Kristjan wasn't a man of commitment. He'd not told her they were exclusive or anything...

And if they cleared the mountain pass...if the first of the winter storms had really gone... what would she do? For her baby's sake?

Was having two parents the best thing? There were plenty of single parents out there doing a fabulous job of raising happy, well-adjusted children. There were children who split their time between parents and they were doing well too. It was what she had originally planned. But everything was different now. Kristjan was invested in their child and she wasn't sure her conscience would be clear if she denied him access to their baby.

But was she too focused on the idea that because she had no parents at all, two were better than one?

Right now, it was all fun and great sex— but what about when that wore off? She was wary of making the same mistake again, but she kept second-guessing herself. What if this *wasn't* a mistake? What if staying in Snowy

Peak with Kristjan *could* be the best thing she ever did?

I still have time to think about it.

She headed to the shops, picked up the meat she would need: smoked lamb, ptarmigan—which was apparently the in thing here in Iceland—and ham. Then she picked up veggies from the market, some *laufabrauð*—leaf bread—from the bakery, and collected the ingredients for a traditional Icelandic rice pudding called *möndlu grautur.* She'd found the recipe after watching a television show, and had thought that a rice pudding made with whipped cream and almonds sounded amazing.

As she shopped, she developed the cosy warm feeling that she was just like everybody else. Domesticated and part of a family, so that she could create an amazing Icelandic Christmas for Kristjan. She wanted to do it. He'd put himself out by inviting her to stay—the least she could do was cook. And it felt good!

Back in the UK she'd often spent Christmas alone, cooking for one, or had made sure she took the day shift at work and had Christmas lunch there when she could grab it. Sometimes it had been nice. Other times Christmas had just proved to her what she *didn't* have.

Even the one Christmas she'd shared with Mark had been so…restrictive. They'd been on honeymoon, for goodness' sake, and yet Mark had wanted a Christmas like the ones he was used to having at home with his family. Because she had no family traditions of her own she had gone along with it, not aware of the reprisals until much later…

This Christmas she wanted to do something nice. Maybe start her own traditions. Because next Christmas she'd have a son or a daughter, and they might only be a few months old, but it would be their most special Christmas ever!

What did she want Christmas to mean to her child?

A special time, just for family, when they would wear matching cosy pyjamas and sip hot chocolate, maybe open just one gift from their Christmas stockings on Christmas Eve! Perhaps they would go to church and light candles and sing carols? Perhaps she would make a Christmas pudding and put a coin in it for one of them to find? Perhaps after Christmas dinner they would go out for a long walk, wrapped up tight in scarves and woolly hats, and perhaps they would have a pet dog to throw sticks for? And she would video the faces of her family as they unwrapped presents and spent the morning playing games and cooking Christmas dinner...and she'd wear a special Christmas apron and...

Listen to me! Perhaps I do love Christmas after all! Perhaps I do love Kristjan?

She checked her watch. Nearly time to head for home.

Home.

It could be. But even if she decided to stay in Snowy Peak, wasn't it presumptuous to assume that she and Kristjan would continue to live together? Wasn't it time she looked for her own place?

There was a local paper in the café that had properties listed in the back. It didn't mean anything...she was just checking out all her options.

She looked them over, circled a couple that could be promising, and then she headed back.

When she got to work, the majority of the staff were dressed in costumes.

Kristjan had on red Santa trousers held up by brown leather braces over a checked shirt, sleeves rolled up at the cuffs, looking like a Santa who'd just spent a couple of good hours in his workshop. The nurses were dressed as elves and angels and shepherds. She felt totally out of place in her normal everyday clothes, so she went and borrowed the elf outfit she'd worn before, when she'd lost that bet with Kristjan.

Christmas music played low in the background of the unit, and it was still—unsurprisingly—as busy as ever. Lots of kids were coming in with viruses, chest infections, and there was one case of chicken pox. She diagnosed a broken arm, a broken wrist, and referred one little boy for an endoscopy because he'd swallowed a coin that was now stuck in his oesophagus. She saw a bad case of nappy rash, consulted with an ophthalmologist because someone had scratched an eyeball on a thorny bush, and admitted one of her young patients she suspected had pneumonia.

She didn't like having to admit children at Christmas, but sometimes it was impossible not to, and she knew the hospital would do its very best to make the kids who were there enjoy the special day.

She was halfway through her shift when she received a call to her mobile phone, and she answered it after scurrying away to a private corner.

'Hello?'

'Dr Bell? It's Kari, from Viktorssons?'

Suddenly it came to her. 'The solicitors? Right!'

'I just wanted to let you know that we have the initial paperwork for you, as you requested, if you'd like to collect it?'

'Really? Oh, that's fabulous! Thank you. Unfortunately, I'm at work now, till late.'

'At the hospital?'

'Yes.'

'I can drop it in for you at Reception on my way home—it wouldn't be any trouble.'

'Kari, you've been an absolute lifesaver! Thank you for doing this. I know it was late notice, but I appreciate it.'

'No problem! Happy Christmas, Dr Bell.'

'You too, Kari.'

She ended the call and bit her lip with excitement, hoping that Kristjan would love what she had done. It had felt right. And, even if things didn't work out between them, it was still a good thing to do.

'Who are you talking to?'

She turned at the sound of Kristjan's voice. He was right behind her.

'No one.'

'All right…'

She could see he didn't believe her. Had he heard who she'd been speaking to?

'I'm finishing now. Heading home. Do you need me to pick anything up?' he asked.

'No, I think I got everything this morning. You could check on the lamb for me. It's in the slow cooker.'

'Will do. What time do you finish?'

'Six.'

'I'll have everything ready for then.'

She smiled. 'I'm meant to be getting it ready for *you*.'

'That's okay. Are we going to the big carol concert at Wonderland later? It starts at nine. The Elf Foundation are singing a couple of songs… I said we'd try to show support if we were free.'

'I'd love to.'

And she meant it. Even though she would have hated the idea of it when she'd first arrived here.

'Great. See you later.' And he leaned forward to kiss her.

One of the male nurses wolf-whistled the pair of them and Merry blushed red. Most of the staff here knew the situation between her and Kristjan and she'd made some very good friends here.

It would be a good place to settle down.

When he got home, Kristjan felt his stomach rumble in anticipation at the aroma when he walked through the front door. Everything was going perfectly. He and Merry were getting on great, and when he'd told her about the mountain pass, she hadn't said a single thing about leaving. That had to be good news, right?

In the kitchen, he got out the steamer and put on some of the vegetables, then made himself a coffee and went into the living room to have a five-minute sit-down.

He saw the local paper on the table and began to browse through it, reading about a court case that was ongoing in Reykjavik and a local dog-sledding endurance race that someone was undertaking to raise money for a brain cancer charity. He went from one story to the next, ignoring the television pages and the financial pages, and was about to close the paper again when he noticed that a couple of properties—local apartments for sale—had been circled.

He sat forward, reading intently.

Apartment for sale, leasehold
Two bedrooms, unfurnished
Parking space and small cellar.

Merry was looking for property? That was great news, wasn't it?

It meant she was planning on staying. It meant that she saw a future for them as a family. That must have been why he'd heard her on the phone with a solicitor!

And it was then that he was suddenly hit with an overwhelming sense of responsibility to get this right that he almost couldn't catch his breath.

How much would it take for him to show that he was able to do this, to be the man they both needed? To be this honoured, to be trusted by her like this, was…unbelievable. All this time she had been alone in the world and now…

Could he do it? Was he capable of opening up his heart and letting them both in so much he wouldn't know where *he* ended and *they* began? If he was going to care for them the way they needed he would have to take action and show them just how committed he was. Prove it to them.

Kristjan got up and went into his bedroom to change.

If Merry could do this and be brave after all she'd been through, then so could he.

Kristjan had lit the candles on the table she'd prepared earlier in the day before going to work. Nat King Cole was playing from the speakers and she emerged to find him pouring some non-alcoholic wine into two glasses.

'To us!' he toasted.

She smiled. 'To us.' And she took a sip, wincing at the tang of the drink. 'Is this battery acid?'

'I hope not. I'd hate to need surgery to repair my stomach lining the day before Christmas.'

'I'll stick to fruit juice, I think.'

She went to the kitchen to pour herself an orange juice and dish up the food into serving bowls for the table. She was looking forward to it. She'd never had ptarmigan before, but assumed it would taste like any game bird. She hoped she could stomach at least a bite of it, not being very keen on meat at the moment.

'I picked you up some noodle soup and a chickpea and vegetable pot pie if you can't stomach the meat,' he said.

'Oh, that's very thoughtful of you. Thanks.'

'No problem. Shall we get started?'

She nodded and smiled as he pulled out her chair for her, and when she was seated comfortably he draped a red cloth napkin over her lap before kissing her on the lips.

'Happy Christmas, Merry.'

'Happy Christmas.'

They clinked glasses once again and, not knowing what to do, she was relieved when Kristjan took the lids off the bowls.

'Shall I serve?' he asked.

'Please.'

He served her a selection of everything and she was determined to try it all. She wasn't keen on the lamb or the ham and though she tried the ptarmigan it wasn't for her—not in her current condition, anyway—so she was relieved to have the alternatives he had so kindly provided.

They took their time over the meal, chatting about the medical cases they'd had in the past, and then Kristjan changed the topic of conversation.

'Tell me about your *best* Christmas.'

'My best one? I think it might be this one,' she said, feeling shy about admitting it.

'Really?' He seemed pleased. 'Didn't you get married at Christmas?'

'A few years ago today. Yes.'

'And that wasn't a good Christmas? Before it all went wrong?'

She shook her head. 'No. But I don't want to think about that time in my life. I've moved on. Everything's changed.'

'For the better?'

'I hope so.'

'So do I. In fact…' He got up from his seat at the table and came over to her, kneeling at her side as he took her hand in his.

What was he doing?

He looked as if he was going down on one

254 THE ICELANDIC DOC'S BABY SURPRISE

knee, and men only tended to do that if they were tying their laces or proposing! And Kristjan's shoes did not have laces…

'Kristjan…'

He put his finger to her lips. 'Please. Let me speak. I've been thinking a lot just lately, and I've come to the conclusion that you and I have something amazing here. We understand each other, we share painful pasts, but more than that we're united in what we want for the future—for our child! Knowing that you're moving here permanently, giving up your old life for us, is—'

What the hell was he going on about?

She hadn't made a decision yet and he was thinking she would just do everything that he wanted? Had he never heard of compromise? Had he never heard of talking things through?

Her chair scraped back noisily as she got to her feet.

'*Stop! Stop it now!*'

A wave of anger washed over her at his presumption. How dared he?

'I never said I was moving here permanently, and you have no right to assume that's what I'm going to do! *I'm* the one in charge of my life! Not you! Do you think you can just get down on one knee and propose to me and assume everything has gone your way? You don't marry someone just because they're having your baby! You marry someone because you *love* them! Have you never listened to a word I've said?'

She threw down her napkin and stormed from the room into the guest bedroom, slamming the door behind her, feeling fury and rage overwhelming her with their strength, along with a feeling of disbelief and injustice!

She'd told him about what had happened with Mark. How they'd got married in a rush, on a whim, with neither of them taking the time to think it through properly and how that had ended for her! Bruised and battered in a women's shelter, swearing off men *for life.*

And he thought proposing marriage to her was a *good* thing to do? On the anniversary of making the worst mistake of her life, he wanted her to make another one? He had *no idea* what he was doing! He was a relationship virgin.

You didn't propose marriage because there was a baby. You married because of love. You married because you couldn't live without the other person! You married because you wanted to be with that person for the rest of your life! To wake up with them and go to sleep with them every single day. To care for them when they were sick. To hold their hand when they were going through something hard. To give them your heart in the palm of your hand, knowing that they would keep it safe for as long as they lived.

He was proposing for all the wrong reasons. For convenience. Because she already lived in his house. Because she already shared his bed. Because she was already pregnant. Because of the baby. He wasn't proposing because he loved her!

And who says I'm staying?

This wasn't real yet. But he was trying to make it so. Trying to fix the holes in their relationship with a giant sticking plaster.

Well, plasters didn't heal anything. They just hid the badness. And if this behaviour, this assumption, wasn't controlling, then she didn't know what was!

Tears trickled down her cheeks as she grabbed her clothes from the wardrobe and threw them on the bed, looking for the wheeled suitcase she'd put away only a few short weeks ago.

Did he not see how she felt? How she would be repeating the past if she jumped straight into a relationship with him? What they had together was fun and, yes, she enjoyed being with him—but was she ready to live a *life* with him?

She stopped to sniff. Wipe her nose.

He'd ruined *everything*!

There was a knock at her bedroom door and then he opened it. 'Merry...'

She saw him see the suitcase, the clothes, the fact that she was packing.

'You're not leaving?'

'Of course, I am! You don't get to have a say in what I do!'

'But, Merry, I—'

She held up her hands. 'I don't want to hear it, Kristjan! Why couldn't you have just...?' She ran out of words, frustrated at his clumsy attempt to advance their relationship into something it wasn't.

'It's Christmas Eve! Please...where will you go?'

'I'll find somewhere,' she said.

THEICELANDIC DOC'S BABY SURPRISE

'But—'

'The mountain pass may be open. I'll ask around. But what I do and where I go is nothing to do with you.'

'You're carrying my child.'

'Oh, I know! I've almost uprooted everything because of it. You persuaded me to stay because of it. You *assumed* because of it. Well, no more.'

'I can't let you wander the streets on Christmas Eve, Merry. And you can't go down that mountain pass if it isn't safe!'

She fastened the suitcase and shrugged on her coat. 'Just try to stop me!' she said, and she barged past, her heart breaking in her fury, storming to the front door and opening it.

Outside, snowflakes gently fell, slow and silent.

She turned. 'I thought you just might be different. But you men… You're all the same.'

And as she closed the door behind her the last thing she saw was the shocked and hurt look on Kristjan's face.

Nat King Cole crooned quietly from the speakers whilst Kristjan sat in his now very empty home, wondering just what the hell had happened.

She'd been planning to move to Iceland. She'd circled some properties in Snowy Peak. Had been speaking to a solicitor. He'd heard her on the phone. You didn't do that unless you were thinking of viewing those properties, and you only viewed properties if you were interested in moving. And the solicitor…? Well, that could have been for anything!

Had he read her wrong? They'd been getting along so well together. He'd thought…

What? What did I think—really?

Okay, perhaps a proposal had been jumping the gun somewhat, but he was new to this relationship malarkey and he hadn't really known what he was doing. But it hadn't really been about the proposal, or love, it had been about showing her that he was committed to her!

But what if she'd never wanted that?

He sat there for a moment, trying to see things from her point of view. She had discovered she was pregnant after a hot one-night stand in Hawaii and had come all this way to another country to tell the father—only to get stranded because of the snow. The father had invited her to stay and to work at his hospital, because he'd known she was a good doctor. But they hadn't been able to keep their hands off one another, and then the father had told her he would convince her to stay.

He had told her, he would convince her...

Was that it? Was that the crux of this matter? Had she felt as if a noose was tightening?

Merry had told him about Mark, about what had happened in her marriage. How her husband had been a controlling man, making all the decisions, telling her what to do.

She'd hated Christmas because she'd made a bad decision at Christmas, to marry a man on impulse. And he, Kristjan, had proposed on Christmas Eve—on impulse!

Oh, boy, am I an idiot!

And now she was out there, traipsing around in the snow, pregnant and with nowhere to go. On Christmas Eve!

In a daze, he walked into the guest room and looked around. The wardrobe doors still hung open, and a couple of coat hangers were lopsided. The chest of drawers wasn't closed properly, and she'd left the book she was reading on her nightstand.

He picked it up and looked at it. Books were special on Christmas Eve in Iceland. Families gave each other books to read the night before Christmas. He'd bought her this book, knowing she wanted it. He'd hoped she was reading it. There was a bookmark. No. It was an envelope. He opened the book for a closer look and saw that the envelope had his name on it.

Merry Christmas, Kristjan!

He sat down on the edge of the bed and opened the envelope to find an official solicitor's letter confirming the fact that Dr Merry Bell was going to be financing, every year in perpetuity, a week at The Elf Foundation for one child who had no family of their own. It was to be called The Bell Prize.

Oh. That was why!

His heart swelled with gratitude that she would do this! That she would join him and provide a special time away for a child at the foundation that he had set up.

She cared. Just as much as he did.

And she was scared. Just as much as he was. He could see that now.

And he'd gone storming in with his big

boots. Thinking that commitment was what she needed to see. But what if he'd been wrong all this time? What if she'd needed to hear something more? Be shown something more?

I should have told her that I love her.

He couldn't lose her. She didn't deserve this and neither did he. He couldn't let things end this way. He had to tell her how he truly felt!

Kristjan didn't even have time to grab his jacket. He simply got up and left, slamming the door behind him, sending a shower of settled snow from his porch down onto his shoulders.

He ignored it.

The cold didn't matter.

What mattered more than anything was Merry.

She'd never imagined that she would be trudging through the snow again, cold and wet, dragging that damned wheeled suitcase behind her the way she had when she'd first arrived, but here she was.

Her first thought when she'd left Kristjan's house had been to tramp right up to the mountain pass and see if she could get down it. But she'd quickly got rid of that idea.

Yes, she would finally be out of Snowy Peak, but it had been a two-hour taxi ride from Reykjavik to get there, and she didn't fancy trudging for hours, seeing if she could hitch a ride from someone in a country she didn't know. And, though she was fairly certain she'd made a huge mistake in leaving Kristjan's house, where it was warm and dry, she didn't want to make another mistake. She knew the pass could be treacherous. It had taken the lives of both of his parents—she would never risk her child's life like that.

I need to find somewhere, but where?

She thought of looking for the B&B, or a pub, but she wasn't sure she wanted to be around people full of Christmas cheer right now—not when she was feeling so miserable and heartbroken. So she decided to head for the hospital. It would be the most sensible thing. Dry and warm and with plenty of beds. She could coop herself up in one of the on-call rooms and eat Christmas dinner in the café, or something.

But she didn't want anyone to know that she was there. She didn't want anyone telling Kristjan that that was where she was. So now she was going the back way to the hospital, slipping in through one of the back doors, using her key pass to get in and a utilities lift to get her up to the staff floor, where she took one of the on-call rooms, locking the door behind her and standing there in the dark.

The room was plain and simple. A bed and a bedside table. A lamp. A phone. In the window was a tinsel star—the only hint that elsewhere people were celebrating.

She didn't put the light on.

She didn't care.

All that mattered was that she was warm and dry. She would stay here until the mountain pass cleared and then she would go. She would not stay with another man who thought he was calling all the shots in her life. Who thought he could impose his will upon her life.

God only knew how he would be once their child came along. And to think she'd thought they could do this without love. Because now she knew you couldn't.

Kristjan! Why did you ruin everything?

Merry lay back on the bed, one hand over her eyes, trying not to cry. She'd thought they had a chance. She really had. They were perfectly matched as friends, as sexual partners, as work colleagues. And she *loved* him! He'd made her fall in love with him!

The connection they shared was like nothing she had ever felt before. She'd kept looking for his faults and had found none—but perhaps his fault was that he couldn't truly see what she wanted? What she needed to hear from him? Perhaps she was the one who had made a mistake? Willing, hoping for him to be different, perhaps she had seen things that weren't there?

All along it had been about the baby. That was what he had said. '*United in what we want for our child.*'

He'd not been proposing because he *loved* her. He'd not been proposing because he couldn't live without *her*!

All along it had been about the baby.

Perhaps he had slept with her because he'd thought that by continuing that pleasure she would be swayed towards staying? Was that it? Had she been used so terribly? Was he like Mark? Acting a certain way to ensnare her and keep her here so he could have what *he* wanted? Had she made the same terrible mistake as before?

The thought sickened her.

She hoped not.

Because if she had then she really didn't think she'd want to see him ever again.

No matter how much it broke her heart.

'Merry? Merry!'

Kristjan trudged through the snow, calling her name, wondering where the hell she'd gone in such a short amount of time. In this cold. In this snow.

He'd wondered for just a brief moment, terrifyingly, if she'd tried to get down the mountain pass—but he'd dismissed that as being ridiculous. She wouldn't do that! It was dangerous and she wouldn't endanger their baby. But in his panic he'd had to check, and so he'd got out the snow sled and raced as fast as he dared to the mountain pass.

There had been no sign of her. No sign of anyone having trudged through the snow there recently.

No. So she had to be somewhere else. *Somewhere.*

He'd driven back to Snowy Peak, calling in at a couple of B&Bs to see if she'd shown up. He went to the hotels and asked, but no one had seen her, and that had been when he thought of The Elf Foundation. She must have gone there! It was the only place she knew, apart from the hospital.

So he'd motored through the snow, ignoring the cold and the strange looks he'd got from people for wearing only a long-sleeved shirt with no coat, and burst through the doors of the foundation.

The kids had been having their read-along. All sitting in a circle, reading their books, surrounded by chocolate and cake and buttery icing-sugar-covered delights.

They'd all looked up at him and what a sight he must have made! In trousers and a thin shirt with no coat, snow on his shoulders and in his hair and his beard.

'Has Dr Bell showed up here tonight?' he'd asked.

'Dr Bell?'

'The woman I came with the other day.'

'Sorry, no. We haven't seen her.'

'Oh.' The disappointment had been overwhelming. 'I'm sorry. I... I can't stay. Merry Christmas.'

'Merry Christmas, Dr Gunnarsson!'

So where was she? The hospital?

Again, he'd leapt onto the snow sled, knowing he had to put this right. Knowing he had to let her know how he truly felt.

The sled had carried him through fine snow and now he was trudging through the thick banks of it that lay up against the shops and doorways. His trousers were soaked, but he didn't care about any of that. It simply didn't matter.

When he got to the hospital, he ran up to a porter who stood by the reception desk chewing on a flapjack.

'Have you seen Dr Bell?'

'No, sorry.'

He ran over to the lifts, to see if he could find her up in the staffroom. The lift seemed to take an age to get there, and when it finally arrived he stood there as it rose upwards, tapping his feet, the breath huffing from his body impatiently, until finally the doors pinged open and he raced down the corridor, passing Agnes, who called out, 'Don't run!'

He slowed to a walking pace and threw open the door to the staffroom, expecting to see

Merry, huddled up on the couch, red-eyed, maybe sipping a hot chocolate or something. But she wasn't there either.

He let out a huge breath.

Where *was* she?

He checked the on-call rooms, rattling at the door handles, but most were empty, or locked, indicating that someone was asleep in there. None had their lights on. And no one had seen her arrive.

She couldn't still be out there, could she? All alone? In the freezing cold?

He'd never forgive himself if something happened to either of them!

I'd never forgive myself... I love her. I can't lose her...

He suddenly realised he might have totally screwed up the one relationship in his life that he *did* want!

Had he, in his fumbling way, ruined what might have been his one true love? Ruined his future with the mother of his baby? He didn't want one without the other, and if he found her and she told him that she was moving back to the UK then he would follow her around the world, if it meant being in their lives. He'd let her call all the shots.

He couldn't do this without her. He couldn't live without her in his life.

I have to find her. I have to tell her everything.

CHAPTER ELEVEN

'MERRY?' THE DOORKNOB rattled slightly, then she heard a curse, and her name repeated at the door of another on-call room farther down the corridor.

Merry huddled underneath the covers, fighting her urge to go to him, praying for sleep to come and steal her away from the turmoil raging in her mind.

She couldn't quite believe that she was in another country, homeless and with no place to go, on Christmas Day. No one to celebrate with. Alone once again.

It shouldn't hurt this much. She'd had many Christmases alone—why should this one be any different?

Because I dared to dream, that's why.

Even though she'd told herself she wouldn't get involved, she had done it anyway. She'd told herself every day not to get too involved with Kristjan, that he wasn't the type of man who settled down, and that even though he might be a good doctor and a good father, it did not mean he would make a good partner for life. He'd not had any practice, had he?

And yet he had somehow got into her heart. Maybe it was the pregnancy hormones— maybe it wasn't. But he'd sneakily got under her defences and she had allowed him in, telling herself it was just sex, that it was sensible— logical, even—to create a positive relationship with her child's father.

Perhaps it was a male thing to think you could call all the shots? Take control? Tell other people what to do? Perhaps because Kristjan hadn't had parents for a long time he was so used to calling the shots in his own life that he thought he could call them in hers?

She thought about that for a moment. It even caused her to sit up in bed.

He's so used to calling the shots in his own life...

Was that it? Was that the key to all this? What had he really done but ask her to consider staying here? For the baby. For him. For *them.*

He wouldn't have asked her to marry him on

a whim—he would have considered it. Kristjan wasn't a man who casually got into relationships.

Have I misjudged him?

But he'd seemed pretty certain she was staying. As if the decision was a done deal. Where would he have got that idea when she hadn't actually confirmed or denied that...? And then she remembered the newspaper she'd brought home from the café. The properties she'd circled so idly, asking herself that if she was going to stay where would she choose? It had been a game, that was all!

But I left the paper on the table. I didn't clear it away. What if he saw it and thought...? Oh, no!

He'd thought she was staying because she'd left evidence to *make* him think that! He wasn't assuming anything about her at all!

And she'd not given him any time to explain. She'd panicked and run, feeling claustrophobic, feeling the ghosts of Christmases past coming to haunt her, telling her she was about to make the same mistake as she had with Mark.

Merry threw off the blankets and grabbed at her shoes. She had to catch up with him!

The suitcase could stay here. It would be safe. All she needed was her coat.

She shrugged into it and unlocked the on-call room door, dashed out into the corridor. It was empty, save for the fairy lights twinkling along the windowsills and a bare trolley bed that was out of use due to a broken bedrail. She ran down the corridor and hit the lift button. It glowed brightly and on the display above the doors she saw that the lift was on the ground floor, but on its way up.

'Come on! Come on!'

When it finally arrived, she dashed inside and pressed the button for the ground floor, twisting her hands over and over as the numbers slowly went from four down to three, to two, to one and then to Ground Floor.

The doors slid open and the music of Christmas assailed her as she ran through the entrance foyer, past the carollers, and as she got to the front door she thought she saw him.

'*Kristjan!*'

He turned, saw her, and she watched him

let out a breath. He looked positively freezing. And soaking wet.

He came running towards her and met her by the huge Christmas tree. He stopped about a metre away.

'I've been looking everywhere for you.'

'I was here.'

'I looked for you in the staffroom—'

'I was in an on-call room.'

'They were all empty or locked.'

'I was there all the time.'

He stared back at her. 'I never meant to assume that you were staying. I never meant to tell you what to do.'

'I know. I know you didn't. I got frightened—by everything. Frightened of making the same mistake. Of rushing into a relationship. Worried that we were together for the wrong reasons.'

'I want you here so that I can be a father, Merry.'

She nodded, knowing she had no right to expect him to love her.

Then he stepped closer, taking both her hands in his.

'But I also want you here because I'm in love

with you and I don't want to be without you. If you need me to move to England with you then I will, because my home will be wherever you and our baby are. We can have an engagement that lasts years if you need to—if you're worried about marriage—or we can carry on as we are! When I tried to tell you before I got it wrong. I'm not used to this. I'm not used to wanting someone. So when you came into my life and threw all my rules and beliefs to one side I wasn't sure what to do.'

She smiled, her heart exploding with happiness. 'You *were* going to propose!'

He nodded. 'Yes. And I know you've done this before, but there's no rush for us to get married. We don't have to elope…we can wait as long as you want if you don't want to marry just yet. I just need you to know that that offer is on the table—always. For when you're ready. For when *you* decide.'

She hiccupped a laugh. He'd just told her everything she ever needed to hear.

'I've already decided, so ask me again.'

He brought her hands to his lips. Kissed them, then got down on one knee.

All around them people had stopped to watch, their faces full of smiles.

'Merry Bell. I love you so much and I want to continue to love you for the rest of my life. Would you do me the honour of becoming my wife?'

Happy tears trickled down her cheeks. 'I will.'

She cupped his face with her hands and brought his lips up to hers, kissing him with great intent. She hoped he could feel just how much she loved him, too! He was her everything!

'We should wait until after the baby,' she said. 'I want to plan a proper wedding this time.'

'We'll do anything you want.'

She kissed him again. So happy! So pleased that she had found him here! So pleased that he had come looking for her! So pleased that she'd been wrong!

Around them, the onlookers clapped and cheered.

'I don't have a ring for you.' He looked uncertain. 'Does that bother you?'

She shook her head. 'Of course not!'

Suddenly he seemed to have a thought, and he swung his plait round to undo the leather tie at the bottom of it before taking her hand in his and tying the leather around her finger.

'There. That will have to do until I can find you the perfect ring.'

She beamed at her leather ring. 'I don't need the perfect ring. I have the perfect man and that's what matters.'

EPILOGUE

One year later

THEIR SON'S HAPPY burbling noises came over the baby monitor.

Merry turned to Kristjan and smiled. 'He's awake!'

She was so excited. Their first Christmas as a family! Einar was six months old and she'd been looking forward to this day ever since he was born.

They got up, putting on their matching Christmas pyjamas and robes, and headed to their son's room.

'Einar! Hello, lovely boy! Merry Christmas! It's Christmas Day!'

Merry scooped her son up into her arms and kissed him on the cheek. He was a big boy, just like his father, and there was nothing she loved more than going to fetch him from his crib each morning.

Einar grinned at her. Some dribble went down his chin before he nuzzled into her neck for a cuddle and she inhaled the delicious baby scent.

'Let's go and see what Santa has brought.'

She had to admit that they might have gone a tad overboard on presents for Einar, and that he was probably going to be more interested in ripping at the wrapping paper rather than in the actual toys, but she didn't care. She was determined to soak up every happy moment with her family.

Kristjan changed his son's nappy whilst she got Einar a Christmas onesie that made him look like a gingerbread man, and then they headed into the living room where the tree awaited, with presents underneath.

It looked like something on a Christmas card. Homely, traditional, festive... There were red and gold twinkling fairy lights, and by the fireplace was a large reindeer made out of sticks and wood, his belly filled with baubles, tinsel hanging from his antlers like icicles.

They all sat down by the fire.

'Look, Einar! Look at all your presents!'

He was sitting up all by himself. He'd started

doing it earlier that week. Because he still had the occasional wobble, they surrounded him with pillows—just in case. He gurgled and chuckled, reaching for a low-hanging bauble.

'Try this, Einar. Your first Christmas present ever.'

She passed him a small, loosely wrapped present and he held it to him and laughed, his one solitary tooth just beginning to show.

Merry tried to show him how to open it, but of course she had to unwrap the whole thing. She revealed a big, squidgy penguin and Einar hugged it tight, dribbling over its head.

'Safe to say I think he likes it,' said Kristjan.

'Yep. Do you think we should do some more, or just let him get used to one at a time?'

'He seems happy with the penguin for now.'

She smiled, looking with adoration at her beautiful blue-eyed son. So like his father.

'I've got a gift for you,' she said to Kristjan, reaching for the gift she'd specially hidden under the tree yesterday.

Kristjan smiled and leaned forward to kiss her. 'Thank you. What is it?'

She laughed. 'Open it!'

He slid his finger under the tape and pulled

it free to find an envelope inside. He opened that and pulled out a cream card, embossed with silver snowflakes. It was a save the date card. The date was in the middle of June.

He opened the card.

Save the Date!
June 14th
The wedding of
Dr Merry Bell
and Dr Kristjan Gunnarsson!

He looked up at her, surprised. 'Really?'

'Yes. Let's do it, Kristjan! Let's get married!'

He pulled her towards him, locked his lips with hers and kissed her under the mistletoe that hung from the ceiling.

Merry felt so happy! This past year had been a whirlwind, what with the pregnancy and getting used to being a mother. But she'd quickly come to realise that she thrived on being part of something—*a family.*

Kristjan made her happier than she had ever thought possible, and he had patiently waited for her to say when she was ready.

Well, now she was. She was more than ready and she wanted the whole world to know it.

'So is that a yes?' she asked, eyes sparkling.

He nodded. 'It's always been yes. I love you, Merry Bell.'

She beamed with happiness and kissed him once again.

* * * * *

LET'S TALK
Romance

For exclusive extracts, competitions
and special offers, find us online:

f facebook.com/millsandboon

📷 @millsandboonuk

🐦 @millsandboon

Or get in touch on 0844 844 1351*

For all the latest titles coming soon,
visit millsandboon.co.uk/nextmonth

*Calls cost 7p per minute plus your phone company's price per
minute access charge

Want even more
ROMANCE?

Join our bookclub today!

'Mills & Boon books, the perfect way to escape for an hour or so.'

Miss W. Dyer

'Excellent service, promptly delivered and very good subscription choices.'

Miss A. Pearson

'You get fantastic special offers and the chance to get books before they hit the shops'

Mrs V. Hall

Visit millsandbook.co.uk/Bookclub and save on brand new books.

MILLS & BOON